Sunrise AT THE
Mayan Temple

Children's Books by
Sigmund Brouwer
FROM BETHANY HOUSE PUBLISHERS

THE ACCIDENTAL DETECTIVES

The Volcano of Doom
The Disappearing Jewel of Madagascar
Legend of the Gilded Saber
Tyrant of the Badlands
Shroud of the Lion
Creature of the Mists
The Mystery Tribe of Camp Blackeagle
Madness at Moonshiner's Bay
Race for the Park Street Treasure
Terror on Kamikaze Run
Lost Beneath Manhattan
The Missing Map of Pirate's Haven
The Downtown Desperadoes
Sunrise at the Mayan Temple
Phantom Outlaw at Wolf Creek
Short Cuts

WATCH OUT FOR JOEL!

Bad Bug Blues
Long Shot
Camp Craziness
Fly Trap
Mystery Pennies
Strunk Soup

www.coolreading.com

Sunrise AT THE
Mayan Temple

SIGMUND BROUWER

BETHANYHOUSE
MINNEAPOLIS, MINNESOTA

Published by Bethany House Publishers
11400 Hampshire Avenue South
Bloomington, Minnesota 55438
www.bethanyhouse.com

Bethany House Publishers is a division of
Baker Publishing Group, Grand Rapids, Michigan.

Printed in the United States of America

Library of Congress Cataloging-in-Publication Data

Brouwer, Sigmund, 1959–
    Sunrise at the Mayan temple / by Sigmund Brouwer
       p.   cm. — (The Accidental detectives)
    Summary: While on an archaeological dig in central Mexico, Ricky, Old Lady Bugsby, and the Jamesville gang investigate the mysterious disappearance of a Mayan girl's father.
    ISBN 0-7642-2577-4 (pbk.)
    [1. Mexico—Fiction. 2. Mayas—Fiction. 3. Indians of Mexico—Fiction. 4. Christian life—Fiction. 5. Mystery and detective stories.] I. Title. II. Series: Brouwer, Sigmund, 1959–   . Accidental detectives.
  PZ7.B79984Su 2004
   [Fic]—dc22
                                                        2004012762

SIGMUND BROUWER is the award-winning author of scores of books. He speaks to kids around the continent in an effort to instill good reading and writing habits in the next generation. Sigmund and his wife, Cindy Morgan, divide their time between Tennessee and Alberta, Canada.

For Olivia
and the sunshine you bring
into this world

CHAPTER 1

This is a story about kites, Sunday School cards, a spooky ten days in Mexico, and instinct. Actually, two instincts. One that belonged to a middle-aged man in a wheelchair who was known as Mad Eddie. And another that belonged to my younger brother, Joel Kidd.

Even now, all I can tell you about instinct is that I have no idea how it works. There isn't much use asking Joel. He'll just shrug and vanish. He's like a ghost, coming and going as quietly as smoke, and disappearing like that same smoke whenever he's finished whatever he just did to scare you into a heart attack.

Instinct.

Somehow from the start—a blue-skied and windy day in spring when I was testing out my new kite—Joel knew. I believe Mad Eddie knew, too. Like maybe they shared a special world and both knew how it would finish nearly six months later on another blue-skied and windy day at the same place—on top of Leighton Hill.

All because of my kite, *Killer Tomato*. . . .

The *Killer Tomato* was red, of course, with wide, curved wings and a streaming tail that flicked and snapped in the slightest of breezes. I'd flown it only once—enough to know that Mike Andrews was making a mistake when he skidded his skateboard to a stop in front of my house. He spun back to face me and our friend Ralphy Zee with his challenge.

"Ricky, I'll tear you to shreds." Mike grinned as wide as a Halloween pumpkin.

Ralphy and I didn't bother getting up from the porch steps. All three of us knew what Mike meant. His kite, *Black Shark*, mean and sleek, was tucked beneath his left arm.

"Actually," Ralphy broke in, "correctly speaking, you'll tear Ricky's *kite* to shreds, not *him*."

"Whatever, Einstein. The *Killer Tomato* won't last more than twelve seconds against this." He pointed at the *Black Shark*.

I grinned back. A person can't help *but* grin back at a guy in mismatched hightop sneakers and a Hawaiian shirt gaudy enough to make your eyes hurt. That was Mike Andrews. Red hair. Freckles. A perpetual New York Yankees baseball cap. And born to try anything that looks impossible.

So that's what I told him.

"The *Killer Tomato* lose its first battle? Impossible."

"That mean we've got a fight?"

"Mike, you're on. Consider your kite doomed."

He nodded at us. "Leighton Hill? Five minutes?"

Ralphy and I nodded back. Two blocks away, Leighton Hill was the highest place in our small town of Jamesville. Hardly any trees. Perfect for sledding in the winter. Perfect for kite flying in the spring and fall when the wind was blowing.

"Go ahead, Ralphy," I suggested. "I'll get my kite."

Ralphy hopped to his feet and joined Mike. They'd have his kite in the air by the time I got there.

Except my kite was not in my bedroom closet where I had left it.

Joel.

It could not be any other reason but him. Silent and terrifying, he's like a personal ghost, the way he follows me everywhere. It seems he can get through locked doors and closed windows. Joel never says much when you do manage to spot him—just stares and watches. He disappears as soon as you turn your head, then reappears when you least expect it. Which is mostly when you're doing something you shouldn't.

To make it worse, Joel has no sense of property ownership—except, of course, for the teddy bear he carries everywhere. Joel does, however, have a great sense for finding any of my things that look fun. Like my kite.

"Moooommmmm!" I hollered from my bedroom. "Will you donate Joel to an adoption agency?"

She told me to quit yelling.

I grumbled all the way out of the house, ran the two blocks to Leighton Hill, and explained why I might be another five minutes. Sure enough, Mike's kite was already a speck in the sky. But Ralphy and Mike understood. Joel terrifies them, too.

It took half an hour, and by the time I found Joel on a quiet side street, it was too late. Too late to meet Mike before supper. Much too late to ever use my kite again.

Joel's efforts might have been funny to a stranger. Unfortunately, it was *my* brother trying to get his teddy bear to fly on the tail of *my* kite, so it was tough to do anything but sigh. Despite the condition of my kite, his determination was so amazing, I stood hidden by some bushes at a corner and watched, half-angry, half-admiring.

This is how it worked. Joel would patiently prop up the kite. Then he'd carefully back away from it and keep the string tight. When he was ten steps away, he'd turn to face forward and run, his tiny legs churning like pistons.

For someone smart enough not to quit, he sure wasn't bright. It would have taken anybody else only one or two runs to realize that the teddy bear was too heavy for the kite to make it into the air no matter how fast you ran.

Not Joel. As I watched, he made five attempts. I knew he had made many more before I had arrived because of one small clue. My kite was torn to shreds from dragging along the asphalt.

He looked so determined and tired, I didn't have the heart to yell. Besides, the damage was done, and yelling wouldn't help.

Instead, after watching for five minutes, I simply walked up and said, "How much money do you have in your piggy bank? Enough to buy a new kite?"

Joel knew I was joking. He grinned through a smudge of dirt and sweat. "Can you make teddy fly?"

I groaned. "Not when I'm busy skinning you alive. Let's go to Leighton Hill and tell Mike there won't be a kite fight today."

When we turned around, there he was. Mad Eddie. Blocking the middle of the street with his wheelchair. Scraggly hair, dark bags under his eyes, gray in his beard, torn dirty shirt, and crippled useless legs. I'd forgotten he lived two houses down.

He ignored me. "You want that teddy bear to fly, kid."

It wasn't a question, and it wasn't directed at me.

Joel nodded eagerly.

Mad Eddie held out his hands for the kite, and Joel brought it forward to him.

"Be here tomorrow at four," Mad Eddie grunted. He removed the teddy bear in silence, handed it back to Joel, and then set the torn kite in his lap.

Then he finally looked at me. "You, too. I'll need help getting up Leighton Hill."

He didn't wait for an answer. Didn't ask if it was okay to take my kite with him. Just scowled and turned his chair to slowly and quietly wheel his way back to his house.

CHAPTER  2

"How does a guy go about trading in a wrecked kite?" I began at suppertime. "Or maybe trading in his brother for something useful, like a new bike?"

Joel showed his lack of concern by slurping a strand of spaghetti.

"Let me guess," Mom said. "It has something to do with the mud you dragged in and out of the house as you screamed and ran around looking for your kite after school."

I'd forgotten about the mud. Maybe it wasn't a great time to ask for a new kite.

Dad slurped his spaghetti.

"Samuel," Mom said. "Why do you think Joel eats that way?"

"Sorry," Dad said. "It's so good I can't help myself."

"Mad Eddie promised to take Joel kite flying tomorrow," I announced. "With my wrecked kite."

Dad stopped his fork halfway to his mouth, and a big roll of spaghetti slid off onto his plate to splatter small drops of sauce across the table.

He wasn't aware of the spilled spaghetti. Or of Mom's quizzical look.

"Mad Eddie?" he blurted. "Inconceivable."

"I agree," I said. "Inconceivable. Impossible. There's no way my kite will ever fly again. That's why I was asking about getting a new one. You see, Joel was—"

"No," Dad interrupted. "Inconceivable that Mad Eddie would take Joel kite flying. He won't even speak to people."

"What did Joel do?" Mom asked.

"That's why I was yelling," I said. "He took my kite, the new one you got me, and—"

Mom sighed. "What did Joel do to get Mad Eddie involved?"

It did not appear that replacing my kite was high on their list of priorities, so I sighed in return.

"Joel tried to fly a kite in front of Mad Eddie's house," I started. Then I explained how Joel had been so determined that not even I could get mad after watching him.

"Flying? That makes sense. I'm just surprised to find out Mad Eddie has a heart left after all," Dad commented. He finally put his fork in his mouth, then looked startled to discover it empty.

"Samuel," Mom said. "Was that a fair statement?"

Dad shrugged. "Steph, remember the guy in high school? Happiest person you could imagine. Always had a joke and a grin. Good athlete, too. And always buzzing with motion. Reminds me of Ricky's friend Mike. Of course, Eddie didn't wear shirts that gave you a headache to look at them."

"Dad!"

"Even back then," Dad said, "Eddie dreamed about flying. Some of us talked about cars or football or university. Eddie just talked jets and planes. Knew them inside out. Nothing flew overhead that he couldn't name. Cessnas, Pipers, Phantoms, you name it."

Mom nodded. "It was kind of cute. Back then—"

"*Way* back then," I reminded her.

"He'll do the dishes, Steph," Dad promised with a grin. "Even if he was telling the truth about your age."

Mom made a face at both of us and continued. "Way back then, my friend went on a date with him once. *She* wanted to walk and hold hands. *He* wanted to show her his aviation history book collection."

Joel finally piped into the conversation. "Ricky has to push him up the hill."

"You'll do it, son?"

My turn to nod. "But I won't have a kite. Of course, it won't be hard to buy a replacement, maybe a little bigger—"

"If Mad Eddie promised to take Joel kite flying, I imagine he'll fix your kite."

My nod became less hopeful as Dad continued.

"Let him take Joel kite flying. It might do Eddie some good. The poor man hates the world because of how he got crippled."

Mom raised her eyebrows. "That might be a snap judgment."

Dad only smiled sadly. "Not really. You know the story. Mad Eddie finally reached his dream. A jet pilot. He had his chance in the Gulf War and flew as many missions as anybody in his squadron. He always promised us he would never get hurt in the air. He was right. It was on the ground he broke his back. A freak accident in a jeep that was bringing him to the airfield one day."

"He's not crazy like people say?" I asked. The picture of his scowl flashed through my mind—along with that of his dirty beard and torn shirt.

"Only bitter, son. Last time I spoke to him was seven years ago. He said I was nuts to believe in God. Nuts to think that there was anything good about this world or life. He hated God then, he told me, and always would. He stays away from everybody, he's so full of hate. Joel must have really touched his heart to get him to come out of the house."

I looked over to see how Joel felt about it. Then looked again.

As usual, he had disappeared. Teddy bear and all.

CHAPTER  3

Joel's teddy bear is his only weak point.

When he's asleep, you can have a band playing in his room or you can wave a steaming, juicy hot dog with mustard under his nose, and he won't wake. Wriggle one paw of his teddy bear and he sits up instantly, staring at you with big accusing eyes.

More times than you can count, Mike and Ralphy and I have needed to get away from Joel, and his teddy bear is our only defense. We'll put it in the dryer, and Joel sits and watches it tumble until the cycle ends—leaving us free to get away without being followed.

When I'm mad at Joel, I remind him that teddy bear stuffing is hard to replace. It gets his attention. But I could never hurt that bear because I remember Joel's face the day Old Man Jacobsen's dog snuck away with it. Joel began digging in all the dog's favorite hiding spots with his plastic toy garden shovel. He wouldn't let me help. Even the dog was smart enough to stay out of sight. Joel's face was muddy with tears and dirt by the time he found the teddy bear. Then he gave it to me to wash and we were both happy.

So naturally, the next day at four o'clock when we showed up in front of Mad Eddie's house, *we* consisted of Joel and me and his teddy bear. Ralphy and Mike had decided there were more important things to do than hang around Mad Eddie, things like counting the blades of grass in an average backyard.

Mad Eddie didn't seem surprised that Joel insisted on getting the teddy bear to fly.

"Tie it to the tail, mister," Joel urged. "Put him up there with the birds."

I groaned. There was my kite, fixed and patched, across Mad Eddie's lap as he sat in his wheelchair on the sidewalk in front of his house. And here was Joel, determined to wreck it again in the same way as yesterday.

Mad Eddie ignored me.

"I know what it's like, kid," he said gruffly to Joel. "Wanting to fly so bad."

Then Mad Eddie glared at me for overhearing, his bloodshot eyes fierce.

I quickly coughed and looked away. *So that's why he's helping Joel,* I thought. *Like maybe having that teddy bear in the sky is part of himself.*

"Hey, grunt." This directed to me. "Get that piano out of your back pocket."

"Pardon—"

"Shake it," Mad Eddie barked as I turned back to him. "Leighton Hill. Double time."

So I walked round back of his wheelchair and began pushing. Joel tagged alongside Mad Eddie and kept pace.

The breeze was strong and into us, and it blew Mad Eddie's long hair behind him so that wisps of it fell across my hands where I held the grips of the wheelchair.

My kite seemed different somehow, and as we walked, I finally realized why. It stuck out on both sides of Mad Eddie's lap. He'd widened it. Mad Eddie, too, like Joel, wanted that teddy bear to fly.

Halfway to Leighton Hill, Joel reached into his jacket and slipped something onto Mad Eddie's lap. I only glimpsed the two cards. They were Sunday School cards, colored in by Joel—probably the only gift he could think of on short notice. But I didn't get to see much of them. Mad Eddie slipped them into his shirt pocket without looking and patted Joel's shoulder.

Ten more minutes of silence brought us to the top of Leighton Hill. There were a few other kite flyers, but none were brave enough to comment at the sight of Mad Eddie, with the gray beard that spilled onto his chest, and eyes of anger that dared any challenge.

"Far 'nuff, grunt," Mad Eddie said to me.

We were at the very top, a small plateau that let us survey the rooftops in all directions. There was town hall and its park in one direction. Our school in another. And above us, the wide pale blue of a sky blown clear of clouds.

"Leave me with sport here," Mad Eddie barked again. "Come back in an hour."

When I returned shortly after five o'clock to climb the well-worn path to the top of Leighton Hill, I saw that Mad Eddie's kite construction had worked.

The *Killer Tomato* flew high and proud, and dangling from its tail was Joel's teddy bear.

Above me and against the lightness of the sky, Joel and Mad Eddie formed a single silhouette on the top of the hill. As I walked closer, I saw them exchanging the spool that held the kite string. One flew it, then the other. And when I arrived it seemed to break into a small and special world.

It seemed that way—private and special—every time I returned to them on top of Leighton Hill after that for the next few months as the school year drew to a close. Because every windy day, Joel would find me as school ended and tug on my sleeve, and I'd take him to Mad Eddie's house. And every windy day, Mad Eddie would be waiting for us in his wheelchair on the sidewalk in front, as if some instinct told him Joel and the teddy bear wanted to go flying.

What he and Joel talked about during those hours is a mystery to me. They'd have that huge kite in the air whenever I returned, with Joel's teddy bear flying high above them. Only once or twice on my return did I catch Mad Eddie with a gentle smile as he watched Joel grinning happily upward at his teddy bear. Once I also caught him looking at those two colored Sunday School cards from Joel. It surprised me that he still kept them. Mostly, though, when I walked up to them they both stopped what they were doing and waited, as if I were a stranger interrupting them.

As for me and Mad Eddie, we barely spoke. In fact, he rarely barked more than four sentences at me each time they flew the *Killer Tomato*.

"Leighton Hill, kid," he'd say, as if I didn't know Joel had brought me over to push his wheelchair up that steep path.

Then on top of Leighton Hill, he'd say, "Far 'nuff, grunt. Leave me with sport here." And after a few seconds, "Come back in an hour."

Their special meetings might have gone on all summer, but on the third day of summer vacation, Joel received an envelope in the mail.

It contained an invitation to Mexico. And flight tickets to match.

CHAPTER 4

"Inconceivable," I muttered. "Absolutely inconceivable."

"That means impossible," Ralphy explained to Mike.

Mike gritted his teeth. "I know that, chowderbrain." He looked to me for help. "Can you inform Ralphy that school ended three days ago?"

I sighed.

Mike ignored my sigh and studied again the long, slim whistle he had pulled from his pocket.

"Dog whistle," he said to Ralphy. "I ordered it from the back of a comic book. They can hear it, but we can't."

To prove it, Mike blew the whistle hard enough to bulge out his eyes. All we heard was the sound of Mike's blowing lips. Nothing from the whistle. But almost immediately the German shepherd two doors down began to howl.

"Cool," Ralphy said. "What's the range on that?"

Mike blew again. Farther down the street, the Murphys' cocker spaniel began to yap with fury.

"Far enough," Mike grinned.

Ralphy shook his head. "The Murphys' dog might be joining in only because the German shepherd got excited. There should be some scientific test we could do to experiment. Like let the dogs quiet down, then blow on it from five houses down in the other direction. From there we can figure out the radius of the range and—"

"Guys, twenty minutes ago Joel opened the first letter he's

ever gotten in his life. And it had six tickets to Cancun, Mexico. With a return date in ten days. The last thing I care about right now is a silent dog whistle."

Mike yawned and stood from where we sat on the back steps of my house. "You know, for midmorning, it sure is hot," he said. "Ricky, I know your mom's at work. Think she'll mind if I go inside and borrow some lemonade?"

"Borrow?" Ralphy asked. "That implies you'll return it later, something I hardly think likely after drinking it."

"Look, Einstein," Mike growled. "I already told you that school was over for—"

I left them there, arguing, and wandered to the big tree in our backyard.

Great day, I thought. *Cool grass to tickle the back of my legs as I sit against this tree to enjoy the shade. A relaxing warm sun. And stupid friends.*

They eventually got the hint and wandered over.

"What's the deal?" Mike asked. "You look grumpy."

"Deal!" I shouted. "My little brother gets an envelope with six tickets to Mexico, expenses for ten days, and both of you stand there going on about lemonade and school!"

Mike and Ralphy exchanged glances.

"He's serious, isn't he?" Mike said with awe in his voice. "It's not another one of his dumb jokes."

Ralphy nodded, "If he *is* serious, that can mean only one of two things."

Trust Ralphy to analyze. In front of a computer, he becomes graceful and calm and serene—a swan on water. Get him away from a computer, and he becomes that swan on land. With uncombed hair sticking straight up, and a wrinkled shirt too large and hanging out the back of his pants, he's a bundle of nerves—and the kind of guy who gets stuck in fences whenever we take shortcuts.

So here I am, completely stupefied by something totally inconceivable, and Ralphy gets ready to launch into a theory.

"Yup," he said. "One of two things. Either Ricky's lost his mind, or Joel really got those tickets."

"Check his temperature," Mike suggested. "Maybe he's got a fever."

"That's it," I said as I stood and dusted my hands. "You guys can start looking for a new friend."

Mike shook his head. "Hang on, pal. We'd love to believe you."

Ralphy nodded. "Except for two things."

"Yeah," Mike said. "The letter and the tickets. You've been babbling about Mexico for the last ten minutes, and not once have you shown us this mystery letter. How do you expect anyone to take you seriously?"

He had a point. I hardly believed it myself.

"I'd love to show you the evidence," I said. "But I made the mistake of giving the letter back to Joel. And he's—"

They groaned and together finished the sentence for me, "—disappeared."

We found Joel on the front porch at Mad Eddie's house. He sat on a short stool alongside Mad Eddie's wheelchair.

Mad Eddie gave his usual grunt of hello as we approached. This time, however, I barely heard it. Mike had been blowing his whistle constantly as we walked—half of Jamesville's dogs were still barking in the background.

As we reached the porch Mad Eddie bent his head back down to continue examining the letter in his hands. A thick envelope rested in his lap.

"See, guys," I said to Mike and Ralphy. "There's the proof."

Mad Eddie raised his head again and stared at me.

"Ever been on an airplane before, kid?" he asked.

"To Disney World once," I began.

Mad Eddie waved his hand as if swatting a fly. His long, messy hair covered half of one eye as it straggled along his cheekbone.

"Commercial jet. Bah. No different from riding a bus."

He brushed away the hair. "I mean a real plane. Where you feel every movement the pilot makes."

I shrugged.

"Well, this looks like your chance." Mad Eddie grinned a crooked, wild grin and held up the letter. "Appears this is legit."

Mike whistled and Ralphy gasped.

Joel smiled.

"Six tickets!" Mike said with another whistle. "Me, Ralphy, Ricky—"

Mad Eddie's face twisted with anger. "Don't forget Joel."

Joel smiled.

Mike spoke quickly. "Of course not. Of course not."

Mad Eddie relaxed.

"Can you read us the letter?" Ralphy asked.

Mad Eddie almost began, then caught himself before he might betray any enthusiasm. He pushed it in my direction.

I cleared my throat and began.

Dear Mr. Kidd,

We are pleased that your background fits our requirements so precisely. As well, you come highly recommended. Please find enclosed the necessary flight arrangements for your group. You will be met in Cancun upon your arrival there.

Signed,
Señor Castillo

There was silence when I finished.

"That's it?" Ralphy said.

"That's it," I replied. "No return address. No phone number."

Ralphy persisted. "Nothing about what they expect Joel to do? Or why he's supposed to bring five other people?"

Joel smiled.

I groaned. "Ralphy," I said, "you can't take this seriously. The letter is obviously a mistake. What can anyone expect Joel to do? He's just barely out of the first grade."

Mad Eddie shook his head. "Somebody invested in these tickets. They must believe in him."

"Inconceivable," I said. "It must be a mix-up. A computer mistake. Somewhere out there is another Joel Kidd—a grown-up—waiting for this letter."

Mike finally spoke again. "Who cares? We'll go down there and find out. Me, Ralphy, Ricky, and"—he finished with emphasis—"we'll be sure to take Joel."

"No, no, no," I said. "This is crazy. Nobody sends tickets to a complete stranger like this, especially if that stranger is six years old. I don't want to be there in person when they discover they wasted six expensive plane tickets on the wrong Joel Kidd."

"Yes, yes, yes," Mike said. "What can they do, shoot us?"

I wasn't worried. Because I knew one thing that would keep us from ever leaving for Mexico. And I told it to Mike with smug confidence.

"Even if the tickets really *were* meant for Joel," I said, "it'll be a million years before our parents let us go to Mexico."

CHAPTER 5

"You're sending us to Mexico with Old Lady Bugsby?" I sputtered the next morning at breakfast. "Absolutely inconceivable."

"Not *Old Lady* Bugsby," Mom corrected me. She looked up from feeding Rachel, my little sister. It was that cereal goo that Rachel always managed to fling in all directions. "Miss Bugsby."

Dad grinned at my astonishment. "What's inconceivable? Mexico? Or the Old Lady—uh—Ethel Bugsby part?"

"Both," I said. Rachel fired out a hand, knocking Mom's spoon to the side. Cereal goo landed on my nose. I wiped it away. Nothing that hadn't happened before. "*She's* been around since before airplanes were invented. And we have no idea who's waiting for us in Cancun. Or what they'll say when they see the wrong Joel Kidd and party."

Dad redirected his grin to Mom. "Stephanie, look at the poor boy's red face. You'd almost think he told Mike Andrews that cows would fly before any parents were—what was the phrase?—insane enough to let all of you go to Mexico."

I *had* said that. Plus I'd told Mike there was so little chance of going that I'd cut his lawn all summer if we did.

"Mike Andrews?" I bluffed. "The name sounds familiar."

"It should," Dad said. "He's the one who spent two hours at Ethel Bugsby's house last evening."

I winced. *When Mike gets an idea in his head . . .*

"He's the one who convinced her that she was much too young to turn down an adventure like this."

Old Lady Bugsby was old enough to be my dad's grandmother.

"And he's the one who convinced her to volunteer as a chaperone. Especially since she's the only adult who could leave Jamesville on short notice."

I finally found my voice. "That's because she's so old she doesn't have a job."

Mom gave me her best motherly smile. Which always means trouble.

"Ricky," she said, "all of us parents got together late last night. We agreed with you. This is crazy. However..."

She waved away any protests I might begin. I snapped my mouth shut.

"Point one," she continued, extending her index finger. "Since the flight leaves tomorrow, there's not enough time to track down the other Joel Kidd to deliver the tickets."

She added her second finger. "Point two. We have no way of reaching the Señor Castillo who signed that letter. No return address. No phone number. There is no way possible to let him know about the mix-up before the flight leaves."

Then her third finger for point three. "But the tickets are legitimate. And nonrefundable. If you guys don't take advantage of them, they'll be wasted."

It's interesting. Late at night, when a guy's staring at the ceiling and planning all sorts of great dreams, anything is possible. Like maybe we'd show up in Mexico and discover Señor Castillo was an evil leader of a revolution, and we'd stop him and become heroes. Stuff like that.

But in the white glare of daylight, reality kicks in. Reality that tells you a bunch of kids would never be able to conquer grown desperadoes armed with machine guns and hand grenades. Reality that reminds you Mexico is thousands of miles away where people don't speak English, and you can't run a couple of blocks home to get away from trouble.

The other part that suddenly hit me as Mom finished speaking was to realize how much we depend on parents to set the rules. And maybe to say no.

I mean, we're always asking for things we know we shouldn't have, things that we think would be fun. Like how I always ask if I can borrow the car. In my night plans, I dream about how cool it would be to show up at school behind the steering wheel to take all my friends for a cruise up and down Main Street. But if Mom or Dad finally gave in and handed me the car keys, I'd probably get nervous and remember the basic problems. Like I've never driven before. Or like I might get in an accident.

What I'm saying is, we always ask for everything we feel like asking, and we depend on them to say no when we need it. And right now, no one was saying no.

So here I was—after spending every minute since Joel got the letter getting mad at how our parents would never let us go on this great adventure—suddenly realizing that Mexico wasn't such a great idea. All because Mom and Dad were telling us we'd be on the plane within twenty-four hours.

"But . . . but . . . this is crazy." I heard myself saying everything I had expected my parents to say. "The tickets are from a total stranger. We don't know who the other Joel Kidd is, what he does, or what Señor Castillo expects him and his team to do! And you're sending a little old lady and a bunch of kids into the jungles of Central Mexico to find out?!"

"Southeast Mexico," Dad said. "The Yucatan Peninsula to be exact." He smiled a fake smile to show he knew he was driving me nuts.

"Señor Castillo could . . . could . . . could be a revolutionary leader!"

"Wrong country, son," Dad said. "Mexico's politics are quite stable."

Mom finally rescued me.

"Ricky," she said, "I forgot to tell you about points four, five, and six. It's something she can afford, and she's decided she wants an adventure, so Ethel Bugsby's already determined that she will offer Señor Castillo half the cost of the tickets when you arrive. After all, it isn't our fault they went to the wrong address. This way, Señor Castillo at least discovers why the other Joel Kidd isn't arriving, and we find out how they got the wrong address. And Señor Castillo doesn't totally lose all his ticket money as he would otherwise."

Dad cut in. "Plus, all of us parents agreed this would be a real treat for Ethel. Life is sometimes lonely for her, and she seemed real excited about this adventure."

Wonderful. I hope she didn't expect us to take afternoon naps when she did.

I realized Mom and Dad were looking at me.

"Point six?" I asked.

"Yes." They grinned together. "Point six."

"We parents could use a break, too," Dad said.

Mom sighed agreement. "Just imagine. The next ten days of summer vacation without worrying about the trouble you and Mike and Ralphy will find in Jamesville."

CHAPTER 6

I'll bet Indiana Jones never began any of *his* jungle adventures waiting on the curb for an antique Cadillac to weave its way up the street so slowly that the two dogs chasing passed it twice.

Which is what I told Mike and Ralphy. They sighed agreement.

Finally the faded blue monster of a car approached near enough for us to see Old Lady Bugsby peering through the spokes of her gigantic steering wheel as she drove.

"That isn't what I think it is," Mike whispered.

"A jungle hat," Ralphy confirmed.

I saw it, too. The brim of her round safari hat touched the top edge of the steering wheel as she strained to see through the spokes.

Eventually the car shuddered to a stop in front of us.

"Joel!" I shouted. Where had he disappeared to? "Jooooeeelll, where are—"

He tapped me on the shoulder. When I landed, he stared at me with mournful eyes, as if wondering how I might not have trusted him to be there.

I glared in return, then dropped my eyes to notice the top three-quarters of a compass casually stuck in his front pocket.

"Joel, where'd you get that?"

"Mr. Eddie."

"I'll hold it for you," I announced. "Looks like you'll lose it."

I held out my hand, and he gave it to me without hesitation. "You'll get it back at the end of the trip," I told him.

"Good morning, troops!" Old Lady Bugsby called as she struggled to push open the car door.

She had once been the town grump. Then a decades-old mystery about her father—one I thought of as the Race for the Park Street Treasure—had been solved, and she'd become less of a grump, especially to kids.

"Good morning," we called back. Mike darted around to the driver's side and helped her.

Old Lady Bugsby's feet hit the pavement with a loud thump, and when she rounded the hood of the car to survey us and our luggage, I understood the strange noise.

Gone was the normal head-to-toe black dress she always wore in public. Gone were the low-heeled, dull black shoes.

Instead, she wore hiking boots—almost knee-high and tightly laced over the top of . . . blue jeans? Above the blue jeans she wore a loose red sweater that matched the color of her . . . lipstick?

She must have caught the shock crossing my face, because she pushed a wisp of gray hair that had become untucked back into her jungle hat and grinned broadly.

"Do you like the new me?" She giggled. "I feel twenty years younger."

"Wow!" Ralphy blurted from beside me. "You *look* twenty years young—"

I elbowed him into silence. I've noticed how women sometimes get touchy when you agree with them on their age or weight.

"You look ready for anything," I said to her.

And I believed it. With that grin flushing her face and the edge of her hat casting a shade that softened her wrinkles, she didn't seem as dried-up as we had always believed. Her long, bony nose didn't seem quite so sharp anymore. And her piercing black eyes not quite so hawklike.

She looked so sweet that right then I was ready to look forward to the next ten days.

"Load the gear," she announced. "Lisa might think we forgot all about her."

"Lisa?" I squeaked.

Mike coughed. "Did I forget to mention Lisa would be going?"

"Somehow it slipped your mind, Mike," I said with a glare.

"Oh. Well, there are six tickets and..."

I did my math. *Me. Joel. Mike. Ralphy. Old Lady Bugsby. And Lisa Higgins.*

"And I wanted some female company," Old Lady Bugsby finished for him. "All this happened on such short notice I couldn't call any of my friends."

"Who would you rather have?" Mike whispered. "One of her old friends, or Lisa?"

I was still trying to decide when Old Lady Bugsby interrupted my thoughts. "I hope you don't mind, Ricky."

"Of course not." I grimaced a smile. "It will be great taking a girl who strikes us out in baseball and beats us in math tests. Just great."

Compared to the leg space in the backseat of an old monster Cadillac, Boeing 757 jets feel like a breadbox. But they are faster. After all, to get to the airport, we had endured three hours of constant horn honking as Old Lady Bugsby and her Cadillac majestically sailed the ninety miles of highway at little more than a crawl. This 757, at least, would cover a thousand miles in almost the same time.

We had already finished the in-flight lunch. Mike—on the far side of Ralphy, who was on my immediate right and already halfway through a book on Mexico he'd started as soon as we were in the air—had minded his manners and managed not to beg the flight attendants for desserts left on other people's trays.

Lisa, Joel, and Old Lady Bugsby sat in the row behind us.

The takeoff had been very smooth, which was good because Mike had talked for half an hour beforehand about the percentage of plane crashes, something he did to scare Ralphy, which worked enough to send Ralphy to the bathroom three times before we even started rolling down the runway.

And now, two-and-a-half hours into the flight, I had a map spread on the tray in front of me.

By looking out the window immediately left, I could see the shiny blue of the Gulf of Mexico far below. We were headed due south and any moment would begin to cross the north edge of the Yucatan Peninsula.

The map showed how the United States and Mexico formed a crooked C around the Gulf of Mexico, much like the C a person would make by curving his forefinger and thumb. And, if the forefinger was Florida reaching down toward the thumb, then the Yucatan Peninsula was that thumb curved upward. Cancun was on the southeast side of the tip of the thumb, where the Atlantic Ocean met the Caribbean.

Thinking about what might be ahead, I didn't know whether to dance with excitement or to moan with dread.

Mexico. Ancient civilizations long buried in deep jungle. The hub-bub of market squares. Mystery and adventure.

Or maybe jail instead.

I tried putting myself in Señor Castillo's position. You've spent all that money on flight tickets only to see five kids and a crazy old lady in a safari hat get off the plane. Maybe his first reaction would be to yell for the police. And Mike Andrews had plenty of stories about how American tourists spent years in jail cells seeing millions of cockroaches and zero lawyers.

And what if Señor Castillo didn't speak English? How could we even try to explain the mix-up? Or how could Old Lady Bugsby try to tell him how she thought paying for half the tickets might be a fair deal for both sides? And how...

"Quit worrying, Ricky."

I banged my knees upward on the lunch tray in fright.

"Jumpy?" Lisa continued from behind me with her head over the top of my seat.

I buried my face in my hands. *How does she read my mind?*

"It's easy," she said. "You always worry enough for the rest of us."

"But I didn't ask how you can read—oh, forget it."

She patted my head. "What can go wrong? We land. Ethel pays Señor Castillo, and we find out why Joel received the tickets. Then we enjoy the rest of the vacation."

Ethel?

"We're friends," Lisa explained in answer to my thought. "She doesn't like it when I call her Miss Bugsby."

"Don't," I said. "Please don't. Don't guess what I'm thinking. Don't tell me what I can worry about. This all seems too strange."

"Human sacrifices," Ralphy said, without looking up from his book.

"What?"

"Human sacrifices. It says so right here. The Maya Indians lived on the Yucatan Peninsula hundreds of years ago and built huge pyramids and tried to ensure a good crop by offering young maidens as sacrifice. Some say on clear nights their dying screams still echo. Others say instead those screams belong to the jaguars as they hunt their prey in the darkness."

Trust Ralphy not to show any fear as long as the scary stuff comes from a book. "Wonderful," I said.

But I'm not sure he or Lisa heard me. As I spoke, my face was buried in my hands again.

CHAPTER  7

When we landed, I didn't need to worry about Joel disappearing, as he does at the worst times.

I worried about his arrest.

"Mister, he's only six!" I protested at the customs booth of the Cancun airport. "Take me instead."

"Six be plenty old for to be mule," the guard grunted in a heavy accent from behind a huge black mustache. His dull blue uniform was stained with large patches of sweat.

"Mule? Mule?" Nothing made sense.

I turned to look for help from the others, who were still in the long line behind me. They appeared as horrified as I felt.

When I looked ahead again, another guard was grasping Joel by his upper arm.

"Hey!" I shouted. "You can't do that!"

When I made a move to help Joel, two others grabbed my arms and lifted me off my feet. I dangled there between them, unable to move ahead.

"You theenk maybe there is something to hide, señor?" the first guard asked me. "Perhaps the leetle compadre is a mule?"

In reply, I kicked sideways and hammered the guard on my left just below his knee with the heel of my shoe.

He sucked air in sharply and clamped my arm tighter. It felt like a shark bite. I stopped kicking.

They set me down as the others led Joel to a side room. The door clicked shut behind them.

"Go through, please." The first guard mocked me with a sweeping bow toward the exit. "We send the leetle one out when we are feenished."

"Not alone," Old Lady Bugsby said.

The guard saw the look of determination on her face and must have decided he would lose the battle. He nodded, then escorted her to the room where Joel had been taken.

Mike, Ralphy, Lisa, and I stood in a glum semicircle as the other passengers filed past, headed toward their luggage on the other side of customs. They all averted their heads, as if looking any of us in the eye meant sharing in our trouble.

"Mule?" I began. "I don't get it."

"That's slang," Ralphy explained. "From what I've read in magazine articles, it means someone who is a carrier, a smuggler, usually of drugs. Mules try it in the strangest of ways. Sometimes in artificial limbs. Other times they'll fill a balloon and swallow it."

Another question took priority. *Where do the customs people think Joel hid drugs or whatever they're seeking?*

Our answer came almost immediately, when a customs guard escorted Joel and Old Lady Bugsby back to us.

Joel walked with a stubborn tilt to his chin. Mainly because his teddy bear was in tatters. After all the times I've threatened to remove the stuffing, it had finally been done. And Joel refused to give them the satisfaction of seeing tears.

When they released his arm, he kicked the biggest guard in the shin, then turned and marched to us.

"Don't worry, Joel," Lisa said quickly with a smile. "I'll fix the bear to be as good as new."

He smiled.

Of course, I'd smile back, too, not that I'd admit it to Mike or Ralphy. While Lisa Higgins can be as much trouble as Joel—the only difference being that she's twelve and doesn't have to sneak up on you to drive you nuts—it's more complicated because, of course, she's a girl. Worse, she's good at sports. What she can't do, she'll practice until she's almost perfect.

And she's pretty. Which catches you off guard once in a while when you're trying to treat her like a pal. She has long, dark hair and eyes as blue as the sky. When she smiles, it's warm sunshine breaking through a thunderstorm; when she's mad, her frown is the thunderstorm itself.

Mainly, though, you remember the smile. So it didn't surprise me when Joel smiled back at her promise to fix the teddy bear.

We had no time to discuss it further.

When we reached our luggage, another voice accented with Spanish reminded me why dread had outweighed excitement during my entire flight.

"Mr. Kidd? Mr. Kidd?"

A short Mexican man—tired and uncaring—shuffled down the wide hallway toward us.

"Mr. Kidd? Mr. Kidd?"

It sounded like *Meester Keyed*.

He wore a baggy, dirty cotton shirt. His dark pants were frayed at the cuffs. And his sandals slapped a slow rhythm as they slid along the floor.

"Mr. Kidd? Mr. Kidd?"

Old Lady Bugsby made the first move. "That's us, Señor Castillo."

I squinted my eyes closed, as if wincing like that would deflect the outrage and confusion sure to follow.

Silence.

When I opened my eyes again, the man was yawning.

"Good theeng that I find you," he said through his yawn. "For a time, I theenk maybe I'm here on the wrong day."

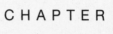

CHAPTER 8

"Inconceivable," I muttered. "Absolutely inconceivable."

"That means impossible," Lisa explained to Mike.

"Really?" Mike commented in a voice laced with sarcasm. "No one's ever explained that to me before."

Mike glared at Ralphy as if daring him to comment, then shook his head in disgust and kept pace as all of us followed Señor Castillo down the hallway to where the airport opened into a mini-mall crowded with souvenir shops.

It was not difficult to keep up with Señor Castillo and his unenthusiastic shuffle. But it was difficult to dodge the hundreds of passengers filling this part of the airport, too many armed with bulging travel bags that swung dangerously in all directions.

I had to raise my voice to be heard.

"Inconceivable," I said again. "This guy doesn't lift an eyebrow to see us instead of the other Joel Kidd. And we just follow without asking where he's taking us."

Old Lady Bugsby giggled. "Fun, isn't it? It might take me hours to put this day into my diary."

Real fun.

Maybe we had stumbled into some diabolical international spy plot and were being led away to be tortured for information we didn't have. Maybe the Mexican was pretending not to care who we were but was only faking it because we had failed to give him the right password when we met, and now we were doomed. Maybe they thought Joel was carrying secret micro-film, and that's why he had been searched at customs. Maybe—

"Settle down, Ricky," Lisa said from beside me. "Secret microfilm. Hah."

"How'd you know what I was thinking!"

"Thinking? You were babbling out loud. Save your crazy imagina-tion for the books you want to write someday."

She placed a hand lightly on my arm.

"This will be just fine," she said. "Trust me."

"Trust you?" I shouted ten minutes later. "Trust you?!"

She nodded bravely and yelled something back.

It was difficult to hear her above the roar of the propeller.

"What?" I shouted.

She yelled it again.

"What?"

She folded her hands in prayer and pointed upward.

I nodded agreement. There was no sense in trying more conversa-tion, so I went back to worrying as I waited to board the small airplane in front of us.

We stood in the shade of the airplane wings above us on a minor runway several hundred yards from the main terminal. Even that short distance away, the building shimmered in the overwhelming heat of mid-day. Already I could feel the concrete baking its way through the soles of my sneakers. Drawing a deep breath felt like sucking air straight from a furnace. Sweat plunked downward from my nose like rain.

Worse, I didn't know if I could blame that sweat entirely on the scorch of Mexican summer heat. Too much of the blame might have been fear, fear inspired by the plane which roared and shook and threw streams of black smoke into the air washed back from the single-engine prop at its nose.

The plane's paint—maybe red once—had been blistered away by sun and age. Bolts tinged with rust protruded from the sheet metal of the body. Rust also crept at the edges of the various dents deep enough to cast tiny downward shadows.

Not encouraging.

Yet Señor Castillo, our Mexican guide, was showing his first signs of life, frantically waving us up the steps that led into the dark belly of the plane. Maybe it was because he wanted to quickly retreat to the air-conditioned oasis of the airport building. Or maybe it was because he knew the only way we would get inside this wreck was with strong encouragement.

In the wind of the props, Old Lady Bugsby clutched her safari hat against her head and ducked low as she began to climb into the plane. Joel followed, wisps of the stuffing of his torn teddy bear blowing away. Then Mike, then Ralphy, then Lisa.

I hesitated.

The Mexican shouted something and waved more frantically.

Still I hesitated, glad that I knew my prayers would be heard above any noise. Not that a prayer in that short moment was like a superstitious request for luck. More like admitting that, as always, my life was in God's hands, and this situation was a good reminder of it.

Finally I climbed those short steps.

The smell of the cramped interior of the plane hit me like a plank across the head: stale sweat, old cigar smoke, mildewed rope, and burned motor oil.

From the doorway I could see far enough back to count eight seats, four folded out from each side of the narrow belly, one seat below each tiny window—windows that wouldn't open to let in fresh air.

Behind those seats were boxes and crates and lumpy canvas bags. Everyone was seated except for Old Lady Bugsby, who was in front of me, blocking my way and shouting into the pilot's ear.

Although he, too, was firmly seated, he was half turned from the windshield and controls in front of him and staring into Old Lady Bugsby's face with an expression of shock and anger.

He was obviously an American. Despite the heat that had turned the plane into an oven, he wore a thick leather jacket. He wore a cap that said *Hard Rock Cafe*, and the bill of the cap threw half of his face into darkness. But I could still see a hardness of features that gave me a sudden chill. Hooked nose, heavy chin, and blunt cheekbones. Not someone to mess with.

He looked so tough that I wanted to believe the roar of the engine muted slightly with the door closed behind me was causing me to hear Old Lady Bugsby wrong.

"Young man," she shouted, "these are children!"

She grabbed one of his ears and tugged upward. "And if you use foul language like that in front of them again," she shouted, "I'll rip both of these off."

Nice time for her to surprise me yet again.

"Understand?" she continued.

He stared at her.

"Understand?" She tugged upward so hard on his ear that he had to half lift himself out of the seat.

He brought his fist back, but Old Lady Bugsby refused to let go.

"Understand?"

For a reply, he dropped his fist and tried to nod.

She released his ear, shot him one last angry look, then walked back to her seat with great dignity despite the crouch it took not to bang the ceiling of the plane as she moved.

The scene might have been funny, but this wasn't a movie. And the pilot wasn't laughing.

CHAPTER 9

Was I worried as the small airplane began to taxi down the runway? Not a chance. In fact—as I insisted to Lisa later—I always clench my fists so hard that my fingernails break the skin of my palms.

I could only assume Old Lady Bugsby had asked the pilot for our destination before agreeing all of us would continue our journey. But then I realized even her asking wouldn't have mattered. If the pilot was as angry as he had appeared, there was no guarantee he would tell the truth anyway.

In other words, we were in a plane piloted by someone maybe crazed and certainly upset, with no idea of where we might land or even who was waiting for us.

My nails dug deeper. And I was glad for the distraction of added pain. I would have given three of my teeth—pulled without having my mouth numbed—for the joy of being back in Jamesville doing something as dull as mowing the lawn.

Then the plane gathered speed, and I would have given the rest of my teeth for the privilege of cutting the lawn with only scissors, just to be home. The small plane clattered and shook and skittered and bounced ahead for such a long time I wondered if we had entered a demolition derby.

Then, as if it were agony to peel itself from the ground, our plane pulled upward. The clatter and bounce smoothed into silence, and the roar of the props seemed to fade as we rose.

Freed from the ground, our plane surged with vigor and confidence. We tilted into a turn, and I could see the ground dropping rapidly. My hands relaxed as we swooped upward. For the first time, I noticed fully the pain in my hands, the half-moon cuts in the skin of my palm from my fingernails. And it didn't matter.

I now felt a strange joy in the sensation of flight.

What had Mad Eddie said? That a commercial jet was no different from riding a bus. That in a real plane you feel every movement the pilot makes. And I could.

We continued to rise, and I imagined I could feel the ripples of air sliding past the metal skin, that our plane was a salmon gracefully cutting through the currents as we dipped and bobbed and made our sure way upward to the sun.

I caught Joel smiling and realized he felt the same. And for a moment I understood Mad Eddie's bitter anger to have had this freedom taken from him. I didn't want this flight to end.

Joel's compass, now temporarily mine, indicated we were flying west. Barely a half hour later, the drone of the engine cut slightly, and I knew again the other reason I didn't want the flight to end.

Because our Mexican guide was not Señor Castillo but someone sent by him.

Even without conversation and the chance to compare notes because of the wind noise, I realized now that the short Mexican who had guided us to the airplane had not known whom to expect. Naturally he wouldn't care if the party who responded to his call for Joel Kidd was a group that looked like us. He was just supposed to bring six people to Señor Castillo.

The pilot, though, was a different story.

I had missed his initial reaction as Old Lady Bugsby entered the plane, but I'd heard enough of their conversation to convince me that he knew something was wrong.

Which meant the trouble would happen after we landed. How would Señor Castillo react when he found out my brother wasn't the Joel Kidd he was expecting?

Especially since we had spent the last hour over unbroken jungle. I didn't want to guess how many days it would mean in walking time back to Cancun and the strip of hotels that represented civilization.

The plane banked, and I gasped. A majestic skyscraper reached up from the jungle toward the belly of our plane. I blinked, and my eyes made an adjustment. Not a skyscraper, but a four-sided pyramid in the center of a monstrous clearing in the jungle.

We banked harder to complete our turn, and I saw other large stone ruins scattered in a circle around the pyramid. And even among the trees at the edge of this clearing, there was the dim outline of more structures of stone.

Where are we? There was little time to puzzle.

The plane dropped with the suddenness of a falling piano, and I began to concentrate on worrying about our landing.

The worry was justified, as we hit the runway with a loud bang that threatened to jolt the wings loose. The plane skidded and bounced off the runway and banged down again, until finally it decided to remain earthbound.

We lurched to a crawl, bumping and creaking across the rough concrete for several hundred yards. Then we reached the covered shade of a hangar. The roar of the props cut to silence, and all that was left was the ticking of engine noises.

It was dark inside, and for several heartbeats we all stayed in the private worlds that had been forced upon us by the noise that had made conversation impossible.

Then a snarl of words reached us from the pilot.

"The end of the road, little kiddies." He spoke with savage intensity. "And you'd better do exactly as I say, or it will be the last road you travel."

CHAPTER 10

"Itchy chicken?" Joel giggled from the back of a van ancient enough to make Old Lady Bugsby look like a schoolgirl.

"Chichén Itzá," Ralphy said for the tenth time. "Chichén Itzá."

Joel nodded vigorously, a big smile on his face. "Itchy chicken. Itchy chicken." He tucked his thumbs beneath his armpits and flapped his elbows. "Itchy chicken."

"No," Ralphy began. "*Chichén Itzá*. Ruins of an ancient Mayan city that date back to—"

I interrupted. "Don't bother, Ralphy. The kid doesn't speak much, but if he likes a joke, he won't let go. Like for two weeks when he asked every single night at supper why the chicken crossed the playground."

"Why?" Mike asked.

"Probably just a stage he's going through," I said. But my mind wasn't really on Mike's question. I was still trying to figure out where we were and what would happen next.

The pilot had slammed all of our gear into the empty shell interior of the van, then gave us the choice of walking or getting inside. Then he'd begun to drive, not speaking another word.

The road away from the small airport twisted and turned through dense jungle. The trees—about twice the height of our van—were thick in all directions.

"I mean, why did the chicken cross the playground?" Mike persisted.

I groaned above the squeaking of springs as the van bounced from rut to rut. "Come on, Mike," I said. "Don't we have better things to worry about? Like where"—I pointed to our driver's hunched shoulders at the front of the van—*"he's* taking us."

"To see Señor Castillo, of course," Old Lady Bugsby explained. Her hat was now askew, and more hair had fallen loose, hanging in gray wisps along her face. She appeared tired, and I felt sorry for her, so I didn't voice all my doubts.

Like, if his pilot were this angry, how would Señor Castillo react? And, if the señor didn't appreciate our explanation of why we arrived instead of the expected Joel Kidd and party, how safe was the middle of the jungle?

I hid those worries behind a smile.

"Please," Mike asked. "It's killing me. Why did the chicken cross the playground?"

I rolled my eyeballs. "Tell him, Joel."

"To get to the other *slide*," Joel said happily.

Mike booed. Lisa patted Joel's knee. And I turned to Ralphy, who had been squirming ever since we'd seen the sign beside the weathered wooden buildings near our airplane.

"Okay, encyclopedia head. Spit it out."

"Chichén Itzá. You all saw that sign at the airport. Pronounced here as Chee-CHEN Eet-SAH," he said quickly, as if afraid he might not get the chance to show off his knowledge again. "I spent most of the last day in Jamesville at the library reading about the Yucatan Peninsula. There were a dozen chapters on Chichén Itzá. It's one of the major Mayan ruins in the Yucatan."

He winced, landing hard after a particularly large bump in the road tossed him several inches off his makeshift seat over the van's wheel well. But it didn't stop him.

"The Spaniards conquered the Mayas in the middle of the 1500s, and for centuries many of the significant ruins were buried in the jungle. Then in—" Ralphy frowned with concentration as he tried to recall—"yes, in 1841, an American writer named John Lloyd Stephens published a book that detailed his findings of the then obscure history of the Mayas."

"What was the name of the book?" Mike interrupted with a challenging smirk.

Ralphy blinked once. Then twice, as he retrieved the data. *"Incidents of Travel in Central America, Chiapas and Yucatan."*

"Oh," Mike said, properly humbled.

"Followed in 1843 by *Incidents of Travel in Yucatan,*" Ralphy said without pause. Rarely did we let him spew out this much trivia in one chunk, and he was determined to make the most of it. "That led to a great interest in the area, and many more archaeologists studied these and other Mayan ruins. In the early 1900s—"

"Is that a jaguar crossing the road?" Mike asked.

We all swiveled to look ahead through the grimy windshield.

"Guess not," Mike answered his own question. "So," he continued, "what about the New York Yankees? It's a little early to say, but I think they'll go to the World Series this year."

Ralphy sighed, a sound in the noisy van that I could only guess at by the expression of his face. "Just when I was getting to the good stuff," he said to no one in particular.

Lisa rescued him.

"In the early 1900s . . ." she prompted, giving Mike a dirty look for spoiling Ralphy's fun.

Ralphy beamed. "A guy named Edward Thompson—I forget his middle name, but it was given in the article—bought the land around Chichén Itzá because of the rumored treasure in the Sacred Well."

He paused. Mainly for suspense, to punish Mike. The van jounced another several hundred yards.

"Okay, okay," Mike finally said. "You've got me. What about the Sacred Well?"

"This part was easy to remember," Ralphy replied. "There is very sparse rainfall here and no major river anywhere in the Yucatan. Even worse, there is very thin topsoil over a limestone strata—"

"Strata, schmata. Tell us about the Sacred Well." Mike, rarely patient, was gritting his teeth.

"Strata is rock formation beneath the soil." Now that Ralphy knew he had us, he was in no rush. And I suppose it didn't matter. This road seemed endless, and I was in no hurry for us to meet Señor Castillo. "So with no topsoil and very porous limestone, the rain tended to drain away very quickly. In other words, water was scarce. But in many places the limestone erodes and creates huge holes in the earth called *cenotes.* This well was a cenote so big . . ."

He stopped to check to make sure his audience—us—was giving him full attention.

Satisfied, he continued, "This well was so big and magnificent, it drew worshipers from hundreds and hundreds of miles away."

"How magnificent?" Lisa asked.

"Forget that," Mike said. "What about the treasure?"

"Nearly seventy feet from the rim of the well down to the surface of the water," Ralphy answered. "Or the height of a seven-story building. Of course, the well itself was nearly as wide across as a football field. The water..."

Ralphy blinked again, searching his memory for the information. "The water was nearly another sixty feet deep. In short, from the top of the well to the mud at the bottom, you could put a thirteen-story building."

I whistled.

"The treasure?" Mike asked again.

"Yes, the treasure. This well was so sacred, worshipers threw objects of value down to the water, almost like it was a wishing well. After this guy Edward Thompson bought the land, he dredged the well. The mud at the bottom was twelve feet deep, but he persevered and began to find those valuable objects."

"Like what, Ralphy?" Even Old Lady Bugsby was interested enough to ask questions.

Ralphy gloried in the attention. "Bells of gold, beads of jade, rings of copper, and beautifully engraved gold disks. Priceless stuff like that."

Now Mike whistled.

"There's more," Ralphy said.

The van left the narrow track and bounced onto pavement. A car whizzed past us going in the other direction.

That filled me with relief. *A two-lane marked highway! Other cars! Signs of civilization!*

Then Ralphy's next words—now much easier to hear as the van rode the smooth pavement—chilled some of that relief.

"The Sacred Well also contained hundreds of bones," he said. "Human bones."

"Thanks for sharing that," I told him.

"You're welcome." Ralphy sometimes misses sarcasm, so he finished his story. "The Sacred Well was the site of human sacrifices. Warriors, children, and maidens were thrown into those mysterious depths to appease the rain gods."

Before we could react, our pilot-now-driver spoke loudly.

"History lesson over?" he asked.

That startled us. We hadn't realized how far Ralphy's voice carried.

"Good," the pilot said, taking our silence as agreement. "Because that's exactly where we'll meet Señor Castillo. At the Sacred Well."

CHAPTER

I nearly laughed with relief.

People! People! People! Chichén Itzá had people!

The van moved into a parking lot filled with dozens upon dozens of rental cars and busload after busload of shiny, lobster-skinned tourists.

Our group walked into a modern concrete and tile building that served as entrance and museum to the great scattered ruins of Chichén Itzá beyond—a building with a restaurant, snack shops, souvenir stands, and a bookstore. And hundreds and hundreds of people.

My fears of isolation in the jungle with an insane scientist named Señor Castillo vanished. Our grumpy guide in a leather jacket was just that, a grumpy guide in a leather jacket unhappy about complications. Not some deranged American hiding out in Mexico and earning a living as a pilot for mad scientists.

I was so happy to be among all these people that when a Mexican girl maybe a couple of years older than Joel shyly approached to offer me a map to Chichén Itzá, I gave her without hesitation the five dollars she requested in obviously memorized English.

Our grumpy guide, at least ten steps ahead, then proved himself to be something more—a grumpy guide with good hearing and a streak of violence.

He stopped immediately and walked back to us. He ignored

the throngs of tourists in all directions and slapped the money free from the girl's hand.

"Hey!" I said, echoed by Mike and Ralphy and Lisa as the bill floated downward.

"Hey, what," the man snapped. "These people should know better than to hawk their stuff around me."

The Mexican girl, in a loose cotton dress and with long, braided black hair, stared at the man without comprehension.

"Vamoose," he snarled at her. "Comprendo?"

"I bought that map fair and square," I said. "She didn't do anything wrong."

"Five bucks is a day's wage to some of these people. If they spot you as an easy touch, they'll pester you every step you take around here."

The girl was rubbing the back of her hand where he had slapped it, turning her head back and forth to watch without comprehension as the pilot and I exchanged words.

Old Lady Bugsby stepped forward and picked up the five-dollar bill. "A day's wages?" she asked. "Then I'd like at least a couple more days' worth."

"Quatro," she said softly to the girl, then finished with a long sentence in Spanish.

Spanish? She speaks Spanish? It was to the point where Old Lady Bugsby's surprises were no longer a surprise.

In response, the girl's eyes widened to show them as startlingly black. Then she smiled, a movement that brought prettiness into her wide, dark face. She reached into a pocket of her baggy dress, pulled forth four maps, and accepted a twenty-dollar bill from Old Lady Bugsby.

"I'd like a map, too," Lisa said to Old Lady Bugsby. "Will you tell her that?"

"Me too," Ralphy and Mike said, almost at the same time.

More soft Spanish from Old Lady Bugsby. Another wide smile.

Within moments we all had maps.

"Gracias," the girl said.

"Lunatics," our pilot snarled. "Bleeding-heart lunatics."

He stomped forward without waiting to see if we would follow.

We did, of course. The man who had sent for us by mistake was waiting.

Just before I fell in line behind all the rest, the Mexican girl said something in fast Spanish.

"Pardon me?" I said with hands outward and an upward shrug to show I didn't understand.

She pointed ahead and lifted her eyebrows in question.

"Oh. Where are we going with him?" I shook my head to show the bullying guide wasn't my favorite person either. "To see Señor Castillo."

"Señor Castillo?" It left her mouth as a yelp.

I nodded. "Señor Castillo."

For a moment she froze with both hands over the bottom of her face in horror. She unfroze to frantically reach into her dress pocket, pull loose the money we'd given her, and press it as a crumpled ball into my hands.

Then she fled.

CHAPTER  12

Chichén Itzá.

The grounds stretched out before us in the bright sunshine—flat, wide, and green. It might have been a park somewhere near home, except none of our parks would have been as clearly defined by the wall of jungle that began so abruptly at the edges. And none of our parks would have held the pyramid that so fully dominated the view.

I found out after Ralphy bought another book from the souvenir shop that it is known as the Pyramid of Kukulcan, and it stands nearly one hundred feet high, about as tall as a ten-story office building. It was built from tons and tons of blocks of stone that had been quarried and dragged from miles away. Those stones were so carefully cut and positioned that in many places, even after hundreds of years of weathering, there was not enough room to slide a knife blade between. Those stones had been set in a design almost impossible for today's architects to copy.

Yet the pyramid was over eight hundred years old.

More intriguing than its age was its purpose. Or one of its purposes. The other—as a starting place for the parade of high priests that ended with a maiden thrown as a sacrifice into the Sacred Well—was something I didn't even like to think about.

The first purpose was astronomy. Eight centuries ago—with no telescopes, no computers, not even a slide rule—the Mayas built this incredible structure to let the sun's shadows tell them the exact moment, every six months, that the season changed.

Somehow, without watches or clocks, they designed it so that at that specific moment on March 20 and September 21, the sunlight would project shadows across the steps up the northwest side to form the image of a giant serpent, wavy and dark and one-third of the length of a football field. The same serpent would reappear in shadows of the ghostly light of a full moon on those same days exactly twelve hours later.

Of course, as we first approached, I knew none of this.

I only knew it filled me with an eerie dread, almost as it called to us from across the centuries with the screams of dying maidens and the chants of blood-hungry priests.

Joel felt it, too. He stayed at my side, so close that his flattened teddy bear bumped my hips every third or fourth step.

It helped that tourists dotted our vision in all directions. Yet they, too, were quiet, speaking in whispers as if all of us were conscious of those centuries pressing down upon us.

Our pilot-guide showed no such awareness. He strode angry steps that made it difficult to stay with him. Old Lady Bugsby was already puffing, and I'm sure the heat didn't help, nor did the worry she must have felt to be approaching Señor Castillo—no matter how good our intentions had been in Jamesville when we received the letter.

Despite her lagging pace, we chose to stay with her as the gap between the man ahead and the rest of us began to widen.

Finally he turned around and glared and waited for us to catch up. Then, without speaking, he marched forward again but at a slower pace.

We followed him to the north edge of the clearing, a walk that took ten minutes, then followed him down a path nearly as wide as a road, a path which plunged into the jungle.

"The Sacred Well," Ralphy announced, reading from his map as he walked.

"Where?" Mike asked. He looked in all directions. "I don't see water."

"Ahead of us," Ralphy said.

Our guide grunted agreement, then broke his silence further. "Avoid low trees," he said. "Snakes."

We all looked up and bunched together in the center of the path, making a real good effort to stay with him.

The dappled shade of the trees gave us little relief from the heavy heat. Loud buzzing of insects filled the air. And occasionally there was a bright flash of feathers—parrots. Had the circumstances been different, those flashes of color would have brought exclamations of comment from all of us. Instead, we only whispered among ourselves and remained behind the pilot.

Then we were there, where the narrow road broke and the land dropped in a wide semicircle of cliffs. At the far edge, where the sheer limestone face crumbled, a work party of Mexican men armed with shovels and pickaxes swung occasionally from platforms into the side of the cliff to break away pieces of rock.

Our main attention, however, focused on the water—far, far down and a still surface of green.

What had Ralphy said? Sixty feet deep.

Seventy feet of drop into sixty feet of mysterious darkness. How would you feel, bound and helpless, as priests began to swing you back and forth, ready to cast you into the water? How would you feel, plunging downward and about to shatter that calm surface, to sink—

The pilot's voice brought me from the horror of my thoughts.

"Señor Castillo!" he called loudly to the work force at the far end. "Señor Castillo! I have for you an unpleasant surprise!"

CHAPTER 13

At the sound of Señor Castillo's name, the workers on the far side of the Sacred Well straightened quickly and looked around, then stood at attention while they waited for his appearance.

Who was this man to inspire such fear?

And what would he do to us?

"Señor Castillo!" the pilot called again. "Señor Castillo!"

Finally, from behind the workers, someone rose, a man so tiny that seated in his chair he had been almost invisible.

We had plenty of time to study him as he carefully picked his way toward us along a path around the rim of the well.

If Old Lady Bugsby had been playing the role by wearing a safari hat, this guy had been the one to get to the costume shop first and buy the rest of the outfit.

He wore baggy khaki pants with pockets and button-down flaps up and down both legs. A matching vest with just as many flaps. Shirt beneath, also a light tan color. An equipment belt heavy with filled pouches. And, of course, a safari hat. This one, though, had a fine net hanging to cover his face and neck. He wasn't any taller than Lisa, but the dim features behind the net showed him to be middle-aged.

"Yes, Mr. Jones, what is it?" he cried anxiously when he arrived at the road. "What is this trouble you bring for Señor Castillo?"

His accent told us he was as American as our pilot.

"Rod, you fancy-pants squirt," Jones replied. "How many times do I tell you to cut the mister stuff?" Jones gestured to take in our surroundings. "You're no bellboy. This ain't the Hilton. It's a sweatbox in the middle of nowhere."

"I'm very, very sorry, Mr.—that is, Fred. It's simply that Señor Castillo . . ."

"Scares you, you little twerp. Now, where is he?"

"Merida. Señor Castillo is meeting with officials there in the capital. But, please, don't let my workers know. Otherwise they go even slower. So I cannot help, I'm—"

"—sorry to say. That's how you were going to finish, right? You're sorry to say anything and everything, aren't you?"

The little man bowed his head.

"Boo!" Fred, our pilot, snarled. The little man jumped.

"Why Castillo placed you second-in-command of this dig is beyond me." Fred spit onto the reddish dust at his feet. "And now we got ourselves a problem."

Fred jerked his thumb to point at us.

The little man surveyed us briefly, then dropped his head again. "They appear to be very nice tourists," he said quietly.

"Sure," Fred said. "Real nice tourists. The one with the beat-up teddy bear is Joel Kidd."

The little man lifted his head, then pushed aside the netting to reveal a tiny nose and light crinkles at the sides of his eyes.

"Joel Kidd? And party? Oh dear, there must be a terrible misunderstanding."

Old Lady Bugsby stepped forward. "We believe the same thing. It appeared the only way to resolve it was to arrive here and—"

"Save it, lady," Fred Jones said. He then directed his words to the little man. "Look, Rod—"

Can I believe what I'm seeing?

Old Lady Bugsby had taken another step forward, then mashed the heel of her hiking boot squarely on Fred's toes.

He grabbed his toes and hopped on his good foot and hissed in pain.

Old Lady Bugsby kicked him in the shin of the leg he was using to hop on. I winced at the clunk of boot against bone.

Fred Jones hissed louder.

"Does that get your attention, young man?" Old Lady Bugsby did not wait for an answer. "We've spent three hours in a car, then nearly four hours cramped in a jet, then another hour bouncing around in an old plane, who knows how far squatting in a van, then walking in this heat, and at seventy-eight years of age, I'm tired and ready for a hot bath, which I know I will find—and deserve—as soon as this is cleared up. I'm also tired of your rudeness. So clamp your lips shut while I have a talk with . . ."

I wanted to applaud.

Fred Jones hopped in silence, trying to hold the toes of one leg and rub the shin of the other all at once.

"A talk with . . ." Old Lady Bugsby prompted the tiny man who was staring in fascination at the pain shown by Fred Jones.

"Oh yes!" the tiny man said finally. "With Roderick Kay. That is me." He extended a manicured hand. "My pleasure, Mrs. . . ."

"Miss," Old Lady Bugsby said firmly. "Ethel Bugsby. And if we may spend some time in private—away from this rude man—I'll explain why we chose to redeem the flight tickets that mistakenly reached *our* Joel Kidd. And perhaps you can explain how we might have received them."

"Of course, of course," Roderick Kay said.

Old Lady Bugsby extended her elbow slightly, and Roderick took it gallantly to lead her away from our group. He paused, however, to give one final backward glance of admiration at the now crippled and not-so-tough-looking Fred Jones.

CHAPTER 14

"Mr. Roderick Kay was as baffled as we were that the airplane tickets arrived in Jamesville," Old Lady Bugsby told us that night. "However, he seemed pleased that we had decided to use the tickets instead of letting them go to waste. He seemed pleased to get the money back that I offered. And he was glad that at least we showed up to let him know the tickets went astray."

"No idea at all?" I asked. "What about Señor Castillo?"

Old Lady Bugsby smiled. "That's exactly what I asked. And he told me that indeed Señor Castillo should have an idea. Except he wasn't sure when Señor Castillo would return from the capital of Merida."

Our entire group was sitting in the Mayaland Hotel restaurant, ready for supper to arrive. All my hours of worrying had been wasted. We weren't in some remote jungle camp. Instead, Chichén Itzá was enough of a tourist attraction to have a couple of hotels nearby.

This one sure beat staying in a tent somewhere. We'd just ordered food—Mayan style, lime soup to be followed by maize omelets—and after traveling all day I was hungry enough to consider eating parrot stew.

Hungry as I was, it had been a long day, so even though it was early evening, I was ready to sleep. The drowsy looks around the table showed that I wasn't the only one.

Altogether we had three rooms. Old Lady Bugsby and Lisa

shared one, Mike and Ralphy another, and Joel and I the third. Joel was happy—Lisa had already restuffed his teddy bear and sewn it together. I was happy, too. I was contemplating the simple joy of sinking my head into a soft pillow after a big meal.

As I imagined a great sleep, Ralphy leaned forward and crinkled his forehead in thought.

"There is one thing," he said to Old Lady Bugsby. "Why *did* they expect the other Joel Kidd to arrive? I mean, what is it we're not doing that they want done?"

Old Lady Bugsby rubbed her hands in glee. "I've been saving that as a surprise."

It didn't surprise *me* that she had more surprises.

"Yes?" Ralphy asked with the same serious look.

"Tomorrow, all of us will be amateur archaeologists." She studied our faces. "Apparently the other Joel Kidd is a university professor. He was supposed to be bringing a work crew of five graduate students to help Mr. Kay with this dig."

"Come on," Mike said with a grimace. "Let's not talk about old bones just before supper."

"Old bones?" Old Lady Bugsby said.

Our waitress—with the beautiful, dark coppery skin I had begun to recognize as part of a Mayan heritage and with an equally beautiful and warm smile—arrived with a large tray set with dishes. She placed it on a stand and began to remove bowls of lime soup to set in front of us.

Old Lady Bugsby smiled thanks at her when she finished.

We said grace as soon as the waitress left. I added my own prayer of thanks for surviving the takeoff and landing of the small airplane.

Then Old Lady Bugsby continued. "Old bones? Michael! Archaeology is much more than old bones. We have a chance to dig through history. Layer after layer of soil means century after century of life. Who knows what we might find? Even the garbage of normal living eight hundred years ago tells us how people lived. This is exciting."

"Yes, ma'am," Mike said between slurps with his best cookie-earning grin. "Old bones *and* old garbage. I can't think of anything more exciting."

"Go on with you," Old Lady Bugsby said, trying to frown but not succeeding. "This is a tremendous opportunity. The first city here in Chichén Itzá was built over fifteen hundred years ago. At its biggest, over eight hundred years ago, it held tens of thousands of people and covered several square miles. Tomorrow you get to explore. More than twenty buildings have been found so far. But you never know when the next turn will bring you to another. In fact . . ."

Her voice became hushed. We all leaned forward to listen, but neither Mike nor Ralphy nor I paused from eating our soup.

"In fact, let me tell you about the nearby Grotto of Balankanche. While you were unpacking, I took my bath—" she sighed in fond memory of the relaxation—"and did some reading. The cave had been undiscovered for hundreds of years. Then in 1950 a guide happened to lean against a wall. He fell through and discovered a natural tunnel so low he almost had to crawl. At the end of the tunnel, he discovered a chamber that had been used by priests, which was filled with hundreds of valuable objects left as offerings."

I no longer felt sleepy.

The waitress came by with another tray and began to deliver our omelets.

"And," Old Lady Bugsby said, "all of this huge area is very safe for tourists. We can explore with no fears—unlike some of the early archaeologists who had to travel for days on donkeys through jungle paths to get here."

"That's terrific," Lisa said. She moved her soup bowl ahead to make room for the plate the waitress carried as she leaned past me to reach Lisa. "If we find something valuable, they won't be too upset that the wrong Joel Kidd arrived. And Señor Castillo—"

Halfway across the table, the waitress dropped Lisa's plate. It smashed into shards of china, splashing the tomato sauce of the omelet in all directions.

"Señor Castillo!" the waitress gasped.

Old Lady Bugsby stood quickly and moved to our waitress and put a caring hand on her forearm.

"Are you all right?" Old Lady Bugsby asked.

The waitress recovered, as if that touch and the wondering shock on our faces suddenly reminded her that she wasn't alone.

"Yes, yes," the waitress said. "It's nothing. I . . . I tripped. Please, let me clean this for you."

She hurried away to find a dishcloth and left us in silence.

I remembered the small girl's reaction to Señor Castillo's name earlier in the day, and I began to worry again.

Because I had been closest to the waitress while she served Lisa's plate, and I hadn't seen her stumble against anything.

CHAPTER 15

I dreamed that Señor Castillo was a gigantic muscle-builder with fangs like a vampire and that he chased me through the abandoned ruins of Chichén Itzá in the middle of the night and that I escaped into a chamber in the base of the great pyramid and locked the door behind me and that Señor Castillo had grabbed a battering ram and was running it into the door.

Boom. Boom. Boom.

The battering ram grew louder.

Boom. Boom. Boom.

And then Señor Castillo changed his voice to sound like Lisa's.

"Ricky! Ricky!" he said, trying to fool me in Lisa's voice. "Is everything all right?"

Boom. Boom. Boom.

"Come on," she pleaded. "Answer the door."

Boom. Boom. Boom.

My fuddled brain finally translated that noise into a loud *knock, knock, knock.* Señor Castillo's disguised voice became Lisa's voice in real life. Yes, I was awake. But I was so sleepy, it felt like my eyelids had been velcroed shut.

Knock. Knock. Knock.

"This isn't funny, Ricky! Open up!"

"Yeah, yeah, yeah," I mumbled as I lurched to the door. Travel must have really exhausted me. It would have been easier to wade through mud than to walk those heavy steps in my state of half sleep.

Knock. Knock. Knock.

Joel, that lucky twerp, was still snoring behind me. *Why am I the one who has to answer the door?*

"Ricky—" Lisa stopped as I pulled the door open.

"What is it?" I said. "Can't a guy sleep?"

She quickly looked away and, as she spoke, continued to stare at a distant point down the corridor.

"It's nine in the morning," she said. "Everybody's waiting for you two."

All I could see of her face was the side. What I saw was very red. Then I realized why.

"Eeeep!"

I jumped back and slammed the door shut.

Getting caught in polka-dotted boxer shorts—with nothing else for cover—will do that to a guy.

"Ethel told me more about the project last night," Lisa said to Mike, Ralphy, and me. "Most of it depends on Mexican and American government grants."

Once again we were rounding the corner of the path that opened to the major ruins of Chichén Itzá. It was gloomier today, with gray clouds not quite dark enough to threaten rain. The low sky added to the majestic mystery of the great pyramid ahead.

"That's why Roderick Kay wasn't as upset as you might expect," Lisa continued. "He wasn't paying for the plane tickets in the first place."

"Makes sense to me," Mike said. "How about you, white-legs?"

I growled. Bad enough opening the door in only boxers. But having Mike find out about it later?

I was even grumpier because I had not been able to find Joel's compass. Here we were, about to plunge into the jungle, and I had no way of keeping our direction straight.

I told them that.

Lisa smiled. "What an imagination, Ricky. Chichén Itzá is well explored and well marked. We don't need a compass."

I sulked for a moment. Leave it up to a girl to prefer truth to imagination.

It was difficult, however, to remain in a bad mood. After all, we weren't scheduled to help dig for several hours. And Old Lady Bugsby had agreed to do her sightseeing with Joel. We had maximum freedom.

So we took advantage of it.

In the open area nearest the great Pyramid of Kukulcan, we wandered past a much lower structure, the Temple of Jaguars, to the Ball Court.

I'm not sure how much of it Ralphy saw. His head was buried in a guidebook.

"They played a game called pok-a-tok here," he announced, still deep in the pages. "On a field about the size of a football field."

"Einstein," Mike interrupted. "Look up."

"Right." Ralphy coughed in embarrassment as he finally glanced at our surroundings. "Hey, the guidebook was correct!"

The rest of us just shook our heads, then soaked in the sights.

The field was indeed that big. It was surrounded on the sides by a high stone wall. On each end stood small, crumbling temples.

"Pok-a-tok," Ralphy read, back in his book again. "Like modern day basketball. Except instead of a hoop with a horizontal ring, the hoop was vertical, up and down. They used a six-inch rubber ball. But they couldn't use their hands. They could only kick it or head-butt it through the hoop."

Mike looked down the length of the field and whistled. "Sounds tough." He then grinned. "Did they have a pook-a-took World Series?"

"*Pok-a-tok*," Ralphy corrected. "No World Series. But the heroes and victors were given the privilege of offering their heads as sacrifice."

"What?!"

"Don't worry, Mike," I said. "If you played pok-a-tok like you play baseball, you'd be alive for hundreds of years."

He shot me a dirty look.

I grinned back, happy to get even for his "white-legs" insult.

We then moved on. We walked through the Group of the Thousand Columns—hundreds and hundreds of stone pillars. We saw the steam baths, the marketplace, and a dozen other stone temples. We saw the Temple of The Warriors, the Temple of the Carved Panels, the Tomb of the High Priest, the Temple of the Little Heads, and The Temple of the Owls.

And we saw dozens of Mexican kids hardly older than Joel.

They seemed to be everywhere. Laughing, giggling, and watching us with shy eyes.

Just before noon—when we were expected back for lunch—we also saw the girl who had sold us maps.

"Hello," I called to where she stood with several other kids. "Remember us?"

She looked up. I took a step toward her.

Her eyes widened. She said something in rapid Spanish.

Then she screamed and ran. Her friends followed in full flight.

CHAPTER 16

We arrived at the dig immediately after lunch. We were handed our tools and given hurried instructions by Roderick Kay before he left to answer questions called in Spanish from another work group—after which it took Ralphy less than forty-five seconds to drop a heavy pickax on the toes of the biggest and meanest-looking Mexican of the work crew.

Ralphy stared with horror at his hands, as if he couldn't believe they had betrayed him so quickly. The Mexican stared with horror at his feet, as if just discovering how little protection sandals offer against something as heavy as a sledgehammer. Mike, Lisa, and I stared with horror at the man's broad, scarred face, waiting for an eruption of anger and whatever he might do with the machete that hung on his belt.

The eruption did not arrive.

The Mexican sucked his breath in sharply, rolled his eyeballs upward, and bit his lower lip. Then he smiled sweetly at Ralphy.

"Señor," he said to Ralphy as he grabbed the pickax from the ground with one hand and effortlessly held it out. "This belongs to you. I offer my humblest apologies for my clumsiness. Next time, I assure you, my feet will not be so slow, and you will have no reason for distress on my behalf."

Ralphy accepted the pickax with both hands. And nearly popped his eyeballs with strain as he tried to hold it.

Then the Mexican turned and hobbled with dignity around

groups of men and piles of sun-whitened clay dirt to the far edge of the work area. He sat on a bench near the edge of the clearing that had been hacked from the jungle around us. His low moans were barely audible above the usual clack of parrots, drone of insects, and hum of conversations.

"Just doing your part for international relations?" Mike asked Ralphy. "Promoting goodwill and peace for Americans everywhere?"

Ralphy could not reply. He was still too white-faced with fear. Lisa walked to him and gently removed the pickax from his death grip.

Mike leaned against his shovel, the same way we see municipal employees do it on jobsites back in Jamesville. "Weird. I thought we were dead," he commented. "I mean, I heard the clunk of that pickax landing on the bones of that guy's toes. And he was one mean-looking dude."

"It *was* strange," I said. "Not that anything about this trip has seemed normal."

Ralphy finally found his voice. "And we shouldn't be using shovels or pickaxes, either."

Mike laughed. "I'll say. Especially you. That guy could've torn you in two."

"That's not what I mean," Ralphy persisted. "This is an archaeological site. Everything I've read about this sort of thing tells how careful you have to be."

Mike laughed again. "I'll say. That guy—ooof!"

Lisa smiled with satisfaction at the results of her well-placed elbow in Mike's stomach. "You were saying, Ralphy?" she asked.

"We're supposed to be peeling back layer after layer of soil. Each layer represents a different time period. *Digging* through the layer makes it too easy to destroy anything we might find."

"That's right!" I said. "I've seen photographs in *National Geographic.* All the professors and those kinds of guys are on their hands and knees with little hand brooms, *sweeping* the dirt back inch by inch."

Mike shrugged. "Like we're experts and Roderick Kay isn't?" He gestured around and downward to indicate our surroundings. "Check this setup."

He had a point. We were—as we had expected from the day before—at the far edge of the Sacred Well. A series of platforms lined the steep wall all the way down to the water. Sturdy ladders led up and down from one platform to the next. Various workers handed buckets back and forth. Others dug into the sides of the cliff. On top, near us, other workers sorted through the contents of the buckets.

"Besides," Mike continued to argue, "do you think that Señor Castillo and Roderick Kay could get all these government grants if they didn't know what they were doing?"

Ralphy and I nodded agreement.

Lisa made the smartest comment. "We wouldn't have any questions, would we, if Señor Castillo ever showed up."

That was our schedule for the next three days. Up early to wander around the ruins of Chichén Itzá for the entire morning—sometimes followed by packs of Mexican kids, sometimes not. Then lunch, then hours of digging in the heat that was like a steaming blanket, then supper, then sleep.

In this established routine, there seemed to be little mystery.

Señor Castillo had yet to arrive, but no one seemed upset by our presence. The pilot, Fred Jones, might still have been grumpy, but we never saw him, either.

About the only person we spoke with was Roderick Kay. He was always smiling and always chattering as he bobbed in and out of the various groups of workers at the dig on his tiny, fast-moving legs.

He never seemed upset at the small amount of work that Old Lady Bugsby was able to do in the heat, never irritated at Joel's fierce protection of his teddy bear on the work site.

The only problem with Roderick Kay was that he never had time to answer questions. No sooner would he launch into a patient explanation than a question in Spanish would reach us from another part of the dig and Roderick would excuse himself.

On our fifth day there, we had the first break in our routine.

There was an argument between Ralphy and Mike at breakfast time. I was idly scratching my head and wondering whether or not to try Mexican coffee when the argument started.

"Mike?" Ralphy began around a spoonful of cantaloupe. "I don't mind sharing a room with you. But I wish you'd leave my stuff alone."

"Me?" Mike squawked. "Me? You're the one digging through my suitcase."

"Sure, Mike. What would I want with bright orange undershirts?"

"That proves it," Mike countered. "How would you know about my undershirts unless you were in my stuff?"

"Easy. I found one in my suitcase. Obviously you can't decide which you prefer, mine or yours."

"Hardly—"

Old Lady Bugsby interrupted. "Gentlemen, I think you can blame an outside force for the misunderstanding."

They both swiveled their heads to stare at her.

She nodded. "I believe the culprits are the enthusiastic maids who clean our rooms each day. Why, even Lisa and I sometimes find our belongings rearranged."

Old Lady Bugsby smiled at Lisa. "And I know it's not Lisa. Somehow I don't think she and I share the same taste in clothing styles."

Lisa—beside me—smiled back at Old Lady Bugsby.

I decided to contribute. I scratched my head, then spoke. "I think Old—uh, Miss Bugsby is right about the maids moving stuff around, guys. For two days I couldn't find Joel's compass; then when I had to pick up some pesos I had dropped, I noticed it behind the dresser."

I was about to continue, but I noticed Joel picking at his teddy bear, then scratching his head. Maybe that was contagious, like yawning, but it made me feel like scratching my own head.

So I did.

Then I noticed Lisa alternating stares. First at me. Then at Joel on the other side of me.

"Hey!" I grinned. "This thing about the compass isn't a big deal."

She wordlessly shook her head.

I grinned again and scratched again.

"What?" I said.

Lisa took a deep breath. "Ricky, there are *things* moving in your hair. The same things on Joel's teddy bear."

I reached to my head to scratch. Then stopped halfway there. Because there *were* things moving on Joel's teddy bear.

It took Old Lady Bugsby only one look to figure it out.

Joel and I and the teddy bear had lice.

CHAPTER 17

That night, five minutes after midnight, I was still awake.

Sure, Old Lady Bugsby and the hotel management had decided the lice were caused by unclean stuffing in the teddy bear. Sure, they had disinfected all our clothes. Sure, Joel and I had used a special shampoo again and again and again, just to be sure all the lice were gone. Sure, we had changed hotel rooms.

But how can you be absolutely sure you got every single one of the lice?

I, for one, wasn't.

Every time I closed my eyes, I imagined a little louse on the pillow as it waited for me to fall asleep so it could crawl into my hair and lay a bunch of eggs.

So I didn't sleep.

Instead, every five minutes I snapped my flashlight on and scanned the pillow, hoping to surprise them.

Joel, of course, was fast asleep, even through the scuffles of my sudden and lightning-quick flashes on the pillow.

Then, as if I had a chance of ever sleeping anyway, a slight tap on the door distracted me.

I was smart. I slipped into blue jeans to cover my boxer shorts and threw on a T-shirt as I walked to the door. Then I checked through the spy hole to see who was there.

Nobody.

I shook my head in disgust. *A little late for tricks, isn't it?*

Then I jumped at another tap from the other side of the door.

I quickly looked through the spy hole again.

Nobody.

Another tap.

I opened the door a crack. Still saw nobody.

"Señor" came the whisper.

I looked down and through the crack saw one brown eye staring upward.

I opened the door farther.

"Señor," the little girl whispered again. "Pleeeze."

The girl who sold maps. The girl who ran away.

She reached inside the room and took my hand away from the doorknob, then pulled. I resisted.

"Pleeeze," she repeated and tugged again.

"Why?" I asked.

"Pleeeze." Another tug.

"Why?"

Another tug.

Finally I let her pull me into the hallway.

"Pleeeze," she said, and began pulling me down the quiet hallway.

What was going on?

"No," I said firmly.

She stared at me. She was barely larger than Joel. With bare feet. And big brown eyes that began to fill with tears.

Wonderful.

I amended my refusal. "I mean, no, I need my shoes."

Tears began to roll down her cheeks, taking with them tiny streaks of dirt.

"I'll be right back."

Her continuing tears showed she only understood the word *no* and the shake of my head.

I held up my hand as if asking her to wait and hurried back inside the room to find my sneakers. I bent to tie them, and when I stood and turned, she was right behind me.

I choked back a startled squeak. And silently hoped she and Joel would never become friends, not if she was this quiet and persistent.

Then I let her take my hand and lead me to a fire exit at the back of the hotel.

Yes, it was insane. No one had seen me leave the hotel. I had not left a note. And I was alone in the jungle on a path that led away from a road alongside the hotel, alone with a girl who was probably barely seven years old and who could not understand English. Her vocabulary consisted of the word *pleeeze*, a word she repeated every thirty seconds—which was as often as I tried to stop and pull my hand loose from her grip.

The giant, pale circle of a full moon in a clear sky was nice, but that wasn't much of a consolation. Not when the lights of the hotel disappeared behind us and when the silver light of that moon showed branches and shadows and nothing else but more trees.

And still the girl patiently pulled me forward, deeper and deeper into the trees.

A faraway scream reached us, long and chilling.

I froze. Already I wasn't sure of the direction back to the hotel. What had Ralphy said about screams? From long-dead sacrificed maidens. Or jaguars.

The scream reached us again from somewhere ahead. The girl pulled my hand again, but I was a block of concrete.

Another scream.

"Not to fear," a woman's voice said in my ear.

I'm willing to guess it took five seconds before I landed to stumble backward and finally get a look at the owner of that voice.

"Eees only cat."

Some Mexican woman appears from nowhere right after a scream of horror that would send me ducking even in the safety of a theater and tells me calmly it's only a cat?

"Sure," I said, still stunned. "Only a cat."

She mistook my inability to think or move for something else.

"A brave one, you are," she said. "Most gringos, they hear the beeg cat at night and want to run."

Alone in the jungle with a stranger, I didn't think it was the right time to point out how wrong she was about my bravery level. So I only nodded.

"Good," she said. "A brave one like you is the one we need to stop Señor Castillo."

CHAPTER  18

"Stop Señor Castillo?" I tried a dumb joke, hoping she would send me away. "Stop him? He's going too fast?"

A flash of white teeth. "Gringo. You laugh in the face of danger. I like that."

Wonderful. She was desperate—or crazy—to think that a twelve-year-old kid who couldn't speak Spanish was a knight in shining armor.

I stepped in some mud, soaking my shoes and socks. *Can things get worse?*

Obviously..

Something nuzzled my behind.

"Hey!"

"Shhh. We are yet in this great danger."

The nuzzle became a nip. "But . . ."

The dim light of the moon gave her enough vision to suddenly understand my problem.

"José, you leave this man alone. He have no turnip for you."

I dared turn around to face my attacker and looked a donkey directly in the eye.

By then—after a kid for a midnight caller, a scream from the jungle, a woman appearing from nowhere, and the news that I was now pledged to conquer Señor Castillo—I was ready for anything.

"Hi, José," I said to the donkey with a sigh of resignation.

José returned my greeting with a blast of breath as terrible as sewer air.

"José, he will carry us," the woman informed me. "Our hut is several miles away, and you must be back well before morning."

"No, ma'am," I said.

"It is okay, you stay away all the night? A boy only like you?" Surprise filled her voice. "You Americanos—"

"I mean, no, ma'am, I don't think I should go to your hut."

"I see."

It is this easy to leave?

"Jessica," the woman addressed the small girl. In her Spanish the *J* was soft, so that it sounded like *Hessica.* "No longer should you pray that your father is still alive. Without help, he will never be seen again."

I thought of the girl's large eyes. Then another thought hit me.

"That's not fair," I said. "She doesn't understand English. You just said that to make me feel guilty."

Did I imagine her shrug in that darkness? I thought of how stupid it would be to remain with this crazy woman. Who knew what really might happen at the hut?

"I cannot go," I said in reply to that shrug.

Another shrug.

"Listen. Did you hear that?" she asked.

I strained my ears. A squeal of terror reached me faintly.

Darkness and shadows made it seem like the branches of the trees were clutching at me. I actually wanted to hold the smelly mule for comfort. The squeal rose and died.

"*Esquintla.* A giant rat of the jungle. Fat and slow. The big cats—you Americans call them jaguars—have a great fondness for those giant rats. Remember the scream? A jaguar, hunting in the night. They scream to make the esquintla run. Very easy then to find and kill. Perhaps that jaguar find enough to be filled tonight."

She paused. "And perhaps not. Maybe a slow Americano is easy to find and . . ."

I didn't like the direction of her hints.

"You come with me and Jessica." She smiled. "Or is it that you wish to be left alone here?"

As if joining her in argument, through the dark trees came again the scream of the jaguar. I considered my options.

"Ma'am," I said, "about José. Do I sit behind you and Jessica, or in front?"

CHAPTER 19

"Jessica is not my daughter."

I barely heard her. I was too busy trying not to get caught staring as I stared. The hut around me was just that. A hut. And barely larger than my bedroom.

The walls were made of thick upright poles, stuck in the ground side by side by side and held together with strands of rope. The floor was dirt. The roof was made of grass.

A single oil lamp burned smoky on a short, round table. In one corner of the hut was a hammock. In the other, José the mule. And that was it. From what I could guess, I owned more stuff in the closet of my bedroom than did this entire family.

The woman must have caught my bewilderment.

"Sad, is it not?"

I said nothing.

"My name is Sofia. I myself live in Merida, the capital. There, even women such as I, who clean houses for the rich, can afford to live like kings compared to this."

Jessica moved forward and shyly held the hand of the woman, keeping her gaze down at her feet.

"Yet," the woman brushed back a strand of hair with her other hand, "I am back. After I swore never to return."

"Jessica—she is not your daughter, she is..."

"She is my, how you say..." The woman closed her eyes to concentrate. Lamplight gleamed from her coppery broad cheekbones. When she opened her eyes again, they shone as black as her hair. She looked back at me, her chin level with mine. Something about her was familiar. "She is the . . . the . . . the daughter of my sister."

"Niece," I offered.

"Yes." With her accent, it sounded like *jes*. It was a voice I had heard before. "I learn Eengleesh from the lady whose house I clean. But sometimes the words fail my tongue."

I could not help but smile, even if we were a long donkey ride from the hotel, somewhere in the middle of the jungle, with that same donkey sharing the hut and breathing down my neck. Even with my shoes muddy and my socks soaked.

I asked if I could take them off. Sofia said it was all right. She took the shoes away and a few minutes later brought them back clean. She had cleaned my socks, too, but they were still wet. I slipped the shoes on my bare feet and thanked her. The socks I'd take back to the hotel. If I was ever allowed to go back.

"I return here," the woman said, "because my seester gets word to me about her husband, the father of Jessica."

"She wrote? Telephoned?"

A shake of the head. "Many of us, we do not write. Telephone?" She gestured at the contents of the hut.

I don't feel stupid or anything. I was glad that the dim light hid the red of my embarrassed cheeks.

"No," Sofia explained, "we of the Mayas have our own way of passing word. It does not take long, passed from one to another. Sometimes, yes, we are invisible to the rich people. Men in construction who break their backs working so hard and so long for so little. The women who are maids. But we know more than people think, and we know each other, and word always reaches who it must reach."

I was getting tired of standing, and I shifted from foot to foot.

Sofia whispered something to Jessica in Spanish. Jessica darted from the hut into the night, then returned moments later, struggling with a three-legged stool that she offered me.

"Take it," Sofia said. "She will bring another for me. The men— when they were here—sat outside in the shade. There is enough for all of us."

I sat. Part of me told me I should be more tired. Part of me was wired with electricity. What reason did she have for taking me—a foreign stranger—this far into the jungle in the middle of the night?

In her accented English, she spent half an hour answering that question.

Jessica's father had disappeared nearly six months ago, in the jungle night.

Was it a jaguar? That had been my first question, half-joking and half-serious. It was hard to forget that scream and how the shadows seemed so deep out there.

No. Sofia explained without smiling that the Mayas here believed it had been a giant feathered man. I might have smiled, but her voice then was a whisper, as if she half-feared we, too, might be taken from the jungle never to be seen again.

Kukulcan, she explained. They believed he had returned.

Sofia told me she refused to believe it but that many of her people did. The first Kukulcan, legend said, lived nine hundred years ago. He came from the north. The Mayas threw him into the Sacred Well as a sacrifice, but he did not drown, so they fished him out and gave him the powers of the highest of kings. His name meant *feathered serpent,* and everywhere around statues of a feathered serpent began to appear—statues and carvings that exist to this day.

But now, she explained, some said he had returned. Those who believed in his moonlight appearances and followed his commands would share in his power, it was said. Those who didn't, died strange and cursed deaths or disappeared.

At that point, Sofia's voice became a whisper. "There is even talk of human slavery. I, of course, refuse to believe."

I spoke for the first time in many, many minutes. "What are this Kukulcan's commands?"

Sofia shrugged. "He speaks only to those of us who are the poorest and live closest to the jungle. They are too frightened to pass everything on, even to me, because I am no longer part of the cycle of nature. They say I gave that up by moving to the city."

"No hints?"

"Only that Kukulcan seeks more feathers."

That seemed so crazy that I tried another approach.

"Sofia, can't you go to the police to look for Jessica's father?" Alone in this jungle filled with the strange night noises I had tried to ignore as she spoke, I didn't think it was the right moment to tell her how crazy she and her Mayan friends were. Humoring her, taking her seriously, seemed much smarter.

"Do you see Jessica's mother?" she asked.

I jumped up. Sofia and José had appeared from nowhere with the silence of swooping bats. Had someone just sneaked into the hut?

"She is not here," Sofia continued without comment about my strange behavior. "You do not see her because she, too, disappeared. Why? She spoke of seeking help from the police."

I sat down.

Another scream from the jungle tore the night. This one sounded much closer.

"The big cat. See? This is not the place to be a little one and without someone to look over you. That is why I have returned. That is why I am so careful to bring you here like this, where no one may see us talk together."

I nodded vigorous agreement and shivered total fear all in one motion. *Safer here among hungry jaguars? She must really fear Kukulcan.*

"I am glad you think so, too. You and your friends are the only hope for Jessica's parents and all the others who have been taken."

I blinked back surprise. An old lady and a bunch of kids?

"We cannot go to police. Or more of us disappear. And you . . . you are part of Señor Castillo's group, but not part."

She studied me, waiting for reaction.

I remembered where I had seen her before. And I began to understand.

"You're the waitress from our first night here, the one who dropped the plate."

She nodded. "To hear his name like that. Almost like he follows me everywhere."

I nodded in return. "And that's why Jessica ran away when I mentioned Señor Castillo. Somehow, I believe Castillo shares this evil with Kukulcan."

I didn't finish what I was thinking. That if these people were superstitious enough to believe in a giant feathered man, of course the mention of his name would be terrifying.

"You decided we were not Señor Castillo's helpers?"

"The children watched you for days." I remembered how it seemed they were everywhere during our explorations of Chichén Itzá. "It did not take them long to decide you knew very little. Too little to be on the side of Señor Castillo. Then we also heard about the anger of Fred

Jones, Mr. Pilot for Señor Castillo, and we took great joy in the mistake made that brought you here."

"But why us?"

"Why you and your friends? You are little ones," Sofia said. "Like the Mayas, often people overlook you as no one of consequence. You are the ones who can seek the truth and not be seen."

"What shall we do? We are here only another five days."

"Fred Jones," Sofia said. "He is too much in this. Perhaps he will lead you to the answers."

I nodded. How tough could it be to find out more about an American pilot?

"But you must be very careful," Sofia said. "Even if the legend of Kukulcan is false, too many have already disappeared."

CHAPTER 20

Without a doubt, I should have told Old Lady Bugsby. But I made the mistake of telling myself first that it wouldn't be smart to worry her. So I appeared as bright-eyed as possible the next morning at breakfast and said nothing about the activities of the night before, nothing about the return trip on José that delivered me back to the hotel at two-thirty in the morning.

Instead, I told only Mike and Ralphy in the hotel lobby as Old Lady Bugsby and Lisa and Joel prepared for another morning of sightseeing.

"Cool," Mike said. "We'll spend the rest of our mornings as detectives. No one will miss us."

"Not cool," Ralphy said. "It's only on television that detectives solve the mystery."

"Or stay alive," I added.

Mike shrugged. "I'd like to stay here and argue the point, but you'll have to make your decision now."

He pointed over our shoulders. We followed his gaze out the lobby window.

"Fred Jones," Mike said needlessly, for the man and his unmistakable van were slowly moving up the palm tree-lined road toward the hotel. "See ya later, Miss Bugsby," he called over his shoulder.

With a grin, he sauntered away from us.

I shrugged. Ralphy shrugged.

"Someone's going to have to baby-sit him," I said.

Ralphy shrugged again. "And it's always us, isn't it?"

The door was still swinging shut from Mike's exit when we reached it.

"Jones, the middle of next week?! Is that the best you can do?"

"Yes, sir. I'm afraid so, sir."

"This is your last chance, you dumb grunt. Have that promised squad here by then, or I will personally rip your head off your shoulders and shove it down your neck."

Ralphy and Mike and I crowded one another back into the space between the garbage bin and the wall.

We had followed the van around the hotel, waited until it seemed safe after the slamming shut of the van door, then stayed as close as possible to Fred Jones as he walked to the back of the hotel, near the same exit I had used barely hours earlier to meet Sofia in the jungle.

Then we had pressed back in panic at someone's voice. Unfortunately, that space between the wall and the garbage bin was all that was available. Unfortunately, the bin was full, the air was hot, and our nostrils were in good working condition.

We gagged in total silence and could make only tiny, half-hearted stabs at the persistent flies that chose us for landing areas. The man's voice was too mean; we didn't dare get caught.

"Understand, Jones? We've come too far to bail out now. The help you promised had better arrive today."

"Yes, sir," Jones said meekly.

That was it for the conversation.

Footsteps that we recognized as Jones's approached us across the concrete. We pressed back farther, but we needn't have worried. Jones had his head bowed and was moving quickly. He didn't notice us in the gap.

Mike bolted forward.

Was he nuts?

Mike stuck his head around the side of the garbage bin and looked in the opposite direction of Jones. The click of the closing hotel door reached us shortly after.

Mike stepped back in the gap, a strange expression on his face.

"Here's news," he said. "The guy with a tough voice like an army sergeant?"

"Yes," Ralphy whispered.

"The guy bossing Fred Jones around like he was a kid?"

"Get on with it," I said.

"Roderick Kay. The little guy in a safari outfit."

"No way," I blurted. Roderick Kay was timid, shy. If he ran into a fly, the fly won.

Mike nodded. "Roderick Kay."

Before I could say anything, the van's motor started.

Mike dashed from our spot. We stayed close behind.

"No, Mike!" Ralphy hissed as he saw what Mike had planned.

But it was too late. Mike was already on the bumper of the slow-moving van and holding on to the rack of the spare tire. Ralphy and I had only a couple of seconds to decide whether to stay behind or join him.

Naturally, we were too stupid to stay behind.

CHAPTER 21

I relaxed—only slightly—when I realized we were finally on the road that led to the Chichén Itzá airport. There are no seat belts provided on van bumpers, and the few miles of highway to the turnoff had not been the favorite minutes of my life, even if the highway had been free of traffic.

We began to bounce down the dusty road, coughing and choking on the grit of the dirt that rose in a cloud around our heads.

"Great idea," I tried whispering to Mike, but I succeeded only in swallowing an unhealthy amount of Mexico.

So we rode without speaking.

Then, without warning, as the van slowed for a particularly rough stretch of road, Mike jumped off and rolled to a stop.

It was tiresome to play follow-the-leader with someone like him, but I suddenly realized what Mike had probably known all along.

The van would stop. Soon. And since we knew the only destination could be the run-down little airport ahead, it made more sense to walk the last quarter-mile and sneak up at our leisure than to have to make a desperate attempt to hide by staying on the bumper all the way to the end.

So I jumped, too, and tumbled to a halt.

Ralphy gave a bleat as the van kept moving.

But I wasn't worried. I knew he'd be more scared of being

alone than of hurting himself. Seconds later he launched himself into the air and landed with the grace of a dead elephant.

The three of us dusted ourselves off and began to walk ahead in the heat of a Mexican summer.

How much of a challenge can it be to sneak up on an airport?

Plenty, if you're scared of snakes and you have to leave the road to walk through jungle trees to get around to the back side of the old buildings that line the runway.

We took two steps into the jungle.

"Guys," Ralphy said as he looked upward.

"I know, I know," Mike said. "Snakes hang from trees and wait to jump on people."

"Not that," Ralphy said, even though I noticed his sweat rate had doubled from fear. "It'd be stupid for all three of us to go."

I expected a sarcastic remark from Mike, who always wanted to appear brave. But he said quietly, "It's probably stupid for *any* of us to go."

I knew what he was thinking. Adventures always seem great in the planning stages. Until you're actually there, waiting for a snake to jump on you.

"What I mean is that someone should wait here," Ralphy said. "In case the other two get in trouble."

As usual, Ralphy was right. "You stay," I told him. "You always have nightmares about snakes."

He shook his head. "No, we draw straws. Short one stays. And if the other two don't come back in an hour, he goes for help."

We drew blades of grass because that's all we could find. When we opened our hands, Ralphy held the short one. When we left him, there was mixed relief and pain on his face. And I realized that waiting behind, not knowing what might happen, was probably the toughest job of all.

It didn't take Mike and me long to circle the airport, even if we had to slip and slide among the trees to get there. Mike's sense of direction was so good that I didn't even have to pull my compass out of my back pocket.

We agonized our way forward the last fifty steps to the back of the airport office building.

Is anybody nearby? What will they do if they catch the two of us? And— much too late came the question—*how will we explain this to Old Lady Bugsby?*

Nothing happened. The whine of insects never changed during our approach, the calling of faraway birds kept ringing from all directions, and not a single snake made an appearance.

We reached the back of the building and pressed against the faded cement blocks of the wall. We inched our way around to the side of the building.

Still nothing happened.

Ahead of us, shimmering in the heat, lay the runway. There was the faint smell of oil and diesel gas. But no sounds except those of the sur-rounding jungle.

Then faint conversation reached us.

"Inside," I whispered to Mike.

He nodded.

It was a phone conversation inside the building. There would be a burst of staccato Spanish, then nothing, then another burst. Knowing where the person was made us relax. And that almost did us in.

Stuck against the wall as we were, we were probably as obvious as flies in a sugar bowl. Had Mike not caught a flicker of movement while I was working up the courage to peer in a nearby window, Fred Jones would have spotted us barely seconds later.

Without warning, Mike yanked me back to the corner and pushed me behind him.

"I don't believe it," he said, just barely peering around the corner.

"What?" I whispered.

"A door. He was coming out of the ground through a door!"

Out of the ground?

I dropped to my knees and crawled around Mike so that I, too, could cautiously stick my head around the corner.

There it was at the far end of the runway, the movement that Mike had spotted. Fred Jones was now closing the door behind him—back into the ground.

I fought the urge to rub my eyes. It was a normal-sized door, but set so that when it closed, it became flat on the ground, as if it had fallen there.

If Mike hadn't spotted the movement of the door opening before Fred came out, Fred would have seen us against the side of the building, and who knows what might have happened next. . . .

I shivered.

Fred turned toward the building and began walking in our direction.

We both edged out of sight.

"Did you see that?" Mike hissed. "The top side of the door. Camouflaged. A person could step on it without seeing it first."

For an answer, I stepped back to the edge of the jungle and tugged on Mike's sleeve. Fred's footsteps were already growing louder than I liked.

"Time to go," I said softly.

"But . . ."

"What if he did see us?" I said, "and is pretending he didn't? I want to be gone before he gets close."

Mike nodded reluctantly, and we faded back into the jungle.

CHAPTER 22

Our first priority back at the hotel was simple: water. Glasses and glasses of bottled water to drink. Then each to our own hotel rooms for relief beneath cool, cool showers. Two hours walking back in Mexican morning heat will do that to you.

I sat on the edge of my bed when I finished. It took all of my energy just to pull my blue jeans on after toweling dry. I rested for several minutes, then managed to get into my T-shirt. I flopped back on the bed and absently rubbed the top of my right foot where it was sore from a long walk and friction against my sneaker.

Half an hour until lunch. Then several hours at the dig. Then ... I stared at the ceiling. I didn't want to think about tonight. Because after dark we would have to find out more about the door at the airport.

Insane, yes. But all I had to do was close my eyes to see little Jessica with those big brown eyes. No father. No mother. We had only four days left in Mexico. Even though I didn't really believe we could be enough help to get her parents back, we had to try.

There was so much that didn't make sense.

I kept my eyes closed and thought about it.

The tickets that brought us here. The surprise of discovering it had been Roderick Kay talking so tough when normally he seemed so scared in front of Fred Jones. That strange doorway into the ground.

The legends about a birdman. And a midnight journey into the jungle that left me four hours short of the sleep I had needed.

I drifted from thought to thought, making sense of none of them, and soon I was thinking of nothing and my eyelids grew heavy until . . .

A sharp rap at the door brought me bolt upright from sleep.

I checked my watch.

Five minutes until noon. I'd napped for twenty minutes.

"Give me a break, Mike," I said to the door. "I'll meet you for lunch in a minute."

Another sharp rap.

"Mr. Kidd?" Mike lowered his voice.

Nice try, I thought. *Mike can't fool me that easily.*

The rap of knuckles against wood became insistent. "Mr. Kidd?" Mike's deep voice was muffled through the door.

I grabbed a glass, filled it with water, and went to the door.

"Yes?" I asked, my hand on the doorknob.

"Just a few minutes . . ."

I didn't let Mike finish. I yanked open the door and threw the water at him face high—then gasped in shock at a suited chest that was now soaked dark in front of me at eye level. I slowly looked upward—far too much upward for my liking—at a stern Mexican face half-hidden by a fierce mustache and goatee.

The shorter and older man beside him flashed me a badge.

"Mexican Federal Police," he said. "I think we should talk."

Ten minutes later both of them were laughing so hard the older one sneezed a set of false teeth into his soup. That only made them laugh harder.

Finally, after five minutes, and after everyone in the restaurant was clucking with disapproval, their laughter slowly died to a series of hiccups.

"Don't thay it again," the older one said, trying to pretend there was nothing in his soup. "That little one ith Joel Kidd."

So I didn't say it. I only nodded.

The fierce one, whose suit still had a large dark circle for a bull's-eye in the center of his chest from the water I had thrown, drew a ragged breath and forced seriousness back into his voice.

"How did Señor Castillo react to see the little Joel Kidd?" His question was directed at Old Lady Bugsby.

She smiled calmly and said, "Use a spoon."

"I beg your pardon?"

"Your partner should just use his spoon and fish those teeth out. I've had the same thing happen to me, and there's nothing you can do but put them back in as quickly as possible. It's nothing to be embarrassed about."

The older one looked around, then did as instructed.

"Now," Old Lady Bugsby said, "I'll be happy to answer your questions."

She held up her forefinger and waggled it at the younger one to stop him from talking. "But I'll answer them in trade."

That took all the smiles out of both Mexican Federal Police officers. "Señorita, you are in no position to barter," the older one said.

"No? We haven't done anything wrong."

"You are associated with Señor Castillo."

"Thank you." Old Lady Bugsby smiled.

"Eh?"

"That in itself is interesting information. You regard Señor Castillo to be less than honest."

The younger officer groaned.

Lisa, Mike, Ralphy, and I exchanged proud glances. Old Lady Bugsby wasn't bad for someone that old.

"Why are you investigating him?" Old Lady Bugsby continued.

"We can take you back to the cells in Merida," the younger officer threatened. "And ask our questions there."

"By all means," Old Lady Bugsby invited. "I'm sure the tourist bureau would find that to be great publicity. Mexican police bullying an old lady and five helpless kids."

I thought the officer might choke on his mustache.

The older one merely sighed.

"We trade," he said. "What is it you want to know?"

"For starters," Old Lady Bugsby said, "why are you here?"

"For some time," the older officer said, "our government has had doubts about the project here at Chichén Itzá. Too much money in. Not enough results out."

Old Lady Bugsby nodded. "And your interest in Joel Kidd? Our Joel Kidd or the other one?"

Joel smiled and slurped the last of his soup.

"We thought Joel Kidd was someone else. Someone older."

That answer came as no surprise. When I had introduced them to the Joel Kidd who was my troublesome brother, both officers had been bug-eyed with surprise. Then, of course, the laughter.

"Yes," the younger officer said, then hesitated as he thought through his answer. "We'd heard Señor Castillo was bringing in more help. We thought we'd wait a few days until Joel Kidd had seen more of the operation, then ask our questions."

"What questions?" Old Lady Bugsby said.

The older one shook his head. "Our turn."

Old Lady Bugsby shrugged.

"How did Señor Castillo react to seeing this Joel Kidd?" the older officer asked.

"We don't know," Old Lady Bugsby replied. "We haven't met the man."

"Impossible!" the younger one said.

I had the sudden feeling he wasn't referring to Old Lady Bugsby's comment but rather to something else, something inspired by her answer. We didn't get a chance to continue.

Roderick Kay interrupted us with his approach.

"There all of you are," he said, smiling broadly at us. Then his face darkened with concern and puzzlement. "With guests."

"Mexican Federal Police," the younger one said as he stood. He towered over Kay and made no effort to hide the contempt on his face as he surveyed the safari gear that cluttered Kay from head to toe. "We're looking for Señor Castillo."

Roderick Kay's face whitened, then somehow became even smaller and narrower as he seemed to deflate.

"Oh dear," he said. He seemed ready to cry.

"Oh dear?" echoed the older officer.

Roderick Kay blindly reached for a nearby chair and lowered himself. He began to fan his face rapidly.

"Yes. Oh dear." He pointed to my water. "Please. I need a drink. I feel so faint."

"Get on with it," the younger one said.

Roderick Kay searched their faces as if they might have the answer.

"I've heard the rumors," Roderick Kay said. "I didn't want to believe them. But I haven't seen Señor Castillo in so long. And now that the police have arrived, I fear the worst."

He sipped at the water, then continued in hushed tones. "You see, some of the Mayas on the work site have told me that Señor Castillo was sacrificed to the Sacred Well."

"Sacrificed?" The older officer blurted the word.

Roderick Kay nodded sadly. "Yes. Sacrificed. By a legendary feathered giant of a man known as Kukulcan."

CHAPTER  23

What was discussed after that by Roderick Kay and the federal officers, none of us heard. He immediately led them away from the restaurant and sent word back to us that the dig would be shut down for the afternoon. That was not good news.

It meant that—without work to distract me—I had all afternoon to worry about the coming night. We had planned four and a half hours for the expedition. Two hours each direction. And half an hour checking the door.

I wasn't looking forward to another moonlight walk through the jungle, even if this time Mike and Ralphy would be with me, even if this time we would have flashlights, even if this time we would be armed with the poles we cut during the afternoon.

Sleep was not easy to find, either, not when I knew that my watch alarm would go off at two o'clock in the morning, not when I kept wondering if Ralphy was right in believing that—instead of searching ourselves—we should have told the federal officers about the door.

Trouble was, we had not been able to find either officer throughout the late afternoon or evening. So we had had to make our decision. Search now or let another day go by. And, as Mike had pointed out, maybe the federal officers had already gone back to the capital of Merida.

So I fell asleep to dream of jaguars and snakes that could

fly. I woke to the tinny beep of my alarm and met Mike and Ralphy at the rear exit of the hotel.

At least the cool of night made it easier to walk, even if the top of my right foot hurt slightly from my shoe. We didn't talk much. Along the short stretch of highway, Mike and I were too busy scanning for places to hide in the ditch should the headlights of any car approach. Ralphy was too busy shivering from fear.

Then came the turnoff to the airport road. I took out my trusty compass. "Yup," I announced as I squinted in the moonlight. "North."

"What's that about?" Ralphy asked. "We don't need to know directions when we're on a road."

"Never hurts to know that it's still working," I said. "You never know when—"

I stopped myself. Because I'd almost said *when something might chase you off the road into the jungle.* And that was the last reminder Ralphy needed.

"When what?" he demanded.

"When, um, you can't see the stars to get your bearings. Hey, Ralphy, where is the North Star, anyway?"

He peered upward into the magnificent, deep black sky and searched the stars. It seemed as if a person could reach upward and grab one.

"It's—"

Mike thumped the back of Ralphy's pants with his walking pole. "Get a move on, little dogie."

"Very funny, Mike."

Mike didn't answer. Just turned and marched with determination down the airport road. I didn't like that. Mike usually acts bravest when he's most scared.

"This place is as quiet as a cemetery," Mike whispered as we surveyed the airport buildings, now an eerie white in the moonlight.

"Please," Ralphy jittered, "let's get this over with."

We tried. Except the door was so well hidden it took half an hour to find. And we managed that only because Ralphy stepped on it.

"Guys," he hissed. "Over here!"

We could hardly see him. Which was good. If Ralphy was nearly invisible crouched on the ground, it meant Mike and I were, too, as we slowly ranged back and forth in the flat grass just beyond the end of the runway. We scurried in his direction.

"Listen," he said as we reached him.

He rapped his stick downward. Instead of the solid thud of wood against earth, there was a hollow *twang* of metal.

We squatted beside him and cautiously shone our flashlights downward. Mike reached to scrape away some of the grass woven into the netting on the surface of the metal door.

I grabbed his arm. "Do you want Jones to know someone's been here?"

"Good point," he said. "But where's the door handle?"

Ralphy began patting the door lightly with the flat of his hand. A few minutes later he announced, "Here," then grunted, "It's not locked."

He began to tug upward. The door rose a few inches.

"Come on, guys. Help me."

Mike leaned forward.

A sudden connection of thoughts hit me. *Door not locked. Our banging around.*

"Stop!" I sputtered. They did.

"Let's back off!" Without another word, I turned and ran.

CHAPTER 24

Spurred by my urgency, they followed close behind. I didn't stop until we had reached the deep shadows at the edge of the jungle.

Mike looked at me as if I'd lost my mind. Ralphy looked upward nervously.

"Forget the snakes, pal," I told Ralphy. "Concentrate on the door instead."

"Why?" Mike demanded. "You're giving us heart attacks."

"Why?" I answered. "I'll tell you why. The door's unlocked."

"So? We were just going to go in and out. Nobody'd catch us."

"Stop and think," I said. "Maybe the door's open because Jones is already in there."

That sentence hung there in the silence. Then Ralphy nodded with comprehension. "And we gave plenty of warning by knocking."

"Exactly."

"So what now?" Mike asked.

"Remember that mouse we once trapped in your basement?" I asked.

"Sure," Mike said, puzzled. "It had that little hole in the corner. But I don't get it. Are you suggesting that we take the garden hose and try drowning out whoever is beneath the door?"

Ralphy snickered. "Yeah. And maybe we'll wreck the carpet and get our parents all mad like—"

I sighed loudly enough to cut him off. "Don't you remember the part before the water disaster? When we waited long enough, that mouse would stick his head out just to see if we'd left yet."

It was Ralphy's turn to sigh. "So we've got to stand beneath these trees as prime targets for snakes?"

"I'll blow my dog whistle," Mike offered. "I've been saving it for an occasion just like this. Maybe that will keep them—"

"And bring in every jaguar for miles?" Ralphy sputtered.

"Quiet!" I pleaded. "We'll wait a half hour. If no one comes out by then, it should be safe."

It was safe.

When we returned and pulled open the door, nobody jumped out at us. Good thing. By then, our nerves were stretched so tight we would have collapsed at the slightest movement.

The door opened soundlessly. A quick flash of Ralphy's flashlight showed unpainted concrete steps leading downward. We all paused.

"If we don't do it within five seconds," I finally said, "there's no way I'll be able to stop my feet from running away again."

Ralphy's gulp almost echoed in the clammy silence of the concrete tunnel. Mike flicked his flashlight on and took the first step.

We followed.

Some thirty steps later we reached a sharp turn that led us into a short corridor that ended with an open doorway into more darkness.

Ralphy and I bumped into Mike.

"Knock it off," he growled in a low whisper.

"It's now or never," I whispered back.

Mike straightened his shoulders as he gathered courage, then moved to the open doorway.

We could've taken a thousand guesses each and not come close to predicting what lay beyond. Yet we should have known. Because when we stepped through, the yellow beam of the flashlight bounced off shiny, curved metal a few feet above our heads.

"No way," Mike breathed.

He moved the beam back and the light continued to gleam off more curved metal.

"Too cool," Ralphy said in hushed tones.

I agreed with them both. Sleek and magnificent, it filled most of the giant room. A private jet.

We stepped closer. Above our heads were one wing and one turbine engine. I did the only math I was capable of at the moment. Another wing and another engine on the other side meant this had twin jet engines. I didn't know much about aircraft, but I knew a jet like this probably cost a couple million bucks.

Mike ducked beneath the jet, and seconds later he called in a low voice from the other side, "Check it out, guys."

We did.

On shelves on the far wall, there were dozens of Mayan statues, some half crumbled with age. On the bottom shelf were rows of tubes, and at the end of that shelf, assorted cages.

Ralphy drew our attention in another direction.

"A ramp," he announced. We turned to him and he pointed.

"Heading upward," he said. "And look at the nose of the jet."

Mike and I did, but we didn't understand. All we saw was a small hook protruding downward from the very tip of the nose.

"A ramp and a hook," Ralphy explained. "Add it up."

Mike and I exchanged frustrated looks. "Ralphy," Mike said, "we don't have all night here."

"The ramp's got to lead to the runway," Ralphy said. "But how do you tow a jet up there? Probably a winch. What's the winch attach itself to? That hook on the nose."

He flashed his light around. "There," he announced with triumph. "Hydraulics."

Sure enough, huge hydraulic pistons rested at a forty-five-degree angle at the side of the room. "See where they're attached? Floor and ceiling. I'll bet they move the ceiling upward. Like a gigantic lid to let the jet out. Now—" his voice trailed away as he thought "—how do you activate the hydraulics?"

Amazing how he loses his fear when faced with a scientific or mechanical problem.

"Ralphy!" I grabbed his elbow. "We've seen enough. Let's go."

"Sure," he said absently.

I led him away and up the steps.

There was no one waiting at the top for us, no one waiting behind any of the airport buildings, no one waiting along the road, and no one waiting at the hotel.

We arrived at the hotel barely a half hour before dawn. I was looking forward to a quick shower and a chance to soak the now large bump on the top of my right foot.

Except when I got back to the room, Joel was gone.

On his pillow was a long, colorful feather. And a note.

You and your friends keep your mouth shut about what you saw. Or you won't see your brother alive again.

CHAPTER  25

Ralphy was already asleep by the time Mike answered my soft knock on their hotel door.

"What is it?" Mike asked through a yawn. Awake or not, he was now groggy with lack of sleep from our excursion. But when I told him, fear and adrenaline gave him the same sudden alertness they had given me.

"How?" he asked. "How could they have known so soon we were there?"

"More important," I said, "where's Joel, and what are they going to do to him?"

Mike paced back and forth twice, movement that did not wake Ralphy. "Even if we could find those federal officers, how much help could they give in a jungle as big as the one around us?"

"Exactly," I said. "Jones—and it must be Jones who took Joel—would find out about their search immediately and Joel would . . ." I couldn't even voice the thought.

"Should we tell Old Lady Bugsby?" Mike wondered.

I shook my head. "Nope. Even though she's proven herself to be one tough cookie."

I stopped, puzzled at the way Mike had suddenly begun to frantically shake his head.

"Old Lady Bugsby *is* a tough old cookie," I insisted. "And a pretty cool old lady at that, but she'd insist on calling the police and . . ."

Mike looked ready to cry, and I stopped again as I sensed something behind me. Before I could turn, Mike pointed. And I heard her voice.

"A tough old cookie?" It was hard to tell whether Old Lady Bugsby was amused or not. "And tell me, my *tender young* cookie, why might I insist on calling the police?"

I finally turned. Then edged backward to stand beside Mike for support as she advanced toward us from the doorway I'd left open in my haste to tell Mike about the note.

"And while you're at it," Old Lady Bugsby continued, "humor me. Let an old lady know where you fellows spent the night."

We humored her for the next twenty minutes, but we did not get the chance to finish.

Sofia—in her waitress uniform—burst through the open doorway.

"Oh, there you are!"

All heads swiveled in her direction. Even Ralphy finally woke.

"Jessica, she is missing!" Sofia wailed. She held up a single long feather, an identical match to the one I had found on Joel's pillow. "The feathered serpent, he has taken her!"

Now, as desperate as we had been, Old Lady Bugsby allowed us to begin a search party, but only under specific conditions. That we stayed in the area of the ruins. That we stayed in pairs. That we waited until the ruins opened to the public in another two hours. And that we kept our distance from the slightest danger and reported back to her at the first sign of Jones.

So after waiting until it was safe, we split up—Ralphy and Lisa in one direction, Mike and I in another. Old Lady Bugsby waited back in the hotel for two reasons. One, a phone call ransom message might arrive. And two, despite the note's warning, Old Lady Bugsby was going to try to reach the federal officers who had been here the day before, and failing that, local Mexican police.

Where Sofia went, I had no idea. She had mumbled something about the Mayan network and her own way of helping and then disappeared.

Not that in the confusion of deciding the best plans it really mattered. Joel was gone. We were in trouble if we didn't call the police. We were in trouble if we did. Maybe—just to keep from going crazy by doing nothing—we were just fooling ourselves into thinking that our search of the immediate area would do any good at all, because I don't know what we hoped to find in that short time. As Sofia pointed out, it was more a way of eliminating the obvious areas immediately so that the police would know where to look when they arrived later.

We fanned out through the open ruins at a dogtrot.

First sun had barely cast shadows upon the great pyramid. At any other time it would have been beautiful. Rosy orange light spread across the tops of the trees, and the edge of the sun nudged upward into that glow. The air—cool now before the day's heat—seemed cleansed and vigorous, not steamy and dense. But all that did for me was make it easier to jog.

"Check that direction," I urged Ralphy and Lisa as I pointed past the great pyramid. "Mike and I will scout the Sacred Well."

We turned away from them and began to run down the short stretch of road that led to the well, which had already seen hundreds of human victims.

I tried to block that thought from my mind.

It didn't work.

Hundreds of human victims echoed again and again as we passed beneath the trees at a half-run. *Hundreds of human victims.* All to false gods and for false hopes. And now someone was threatening my brother with the same legends.

But for what?

I fought the image of that long drop from the rim of the well to the calm green surface below. I fought against hearing the sound of a single splash. I fought against thinking of the horror of the slow, silent thrashing against ever deepening water.

And I thought of Joel. *Why him? What is this about?*

Our answer was not at the Sacred Well.

We slowed early enough to catch our breaths and slowly moved forward as we hugged the trees for cover on our approach. In the silent dawn, nothing there stirred. Not even the gaily colored birds swooped in and out. The insects, of course, had yet to rise with the heat.

We moved closer to the dig. There were no workers, the ramps were now wet with dew that sparkled on spider webs and—

A sudden thought.

"Look close, Mike," I whispered. "What do you see?"

"Nothing."

"Exactly. Nothing has disturbed the dew. Or the webs." Joy surged through me. "Nobody has been here!"

My darkest imaginations were swept away as surely as the rising sun began to sweep the shadows around us. Wherever Joel was, it was not below.

"Hurry," I urged Mike. "Back to the rest of the ruins. We'll cover what we can there, then report back to Old Lady Bugsby."

He nodded and we began our return run.

Then, as we broke into the open area at the end of the road, Mike pointed upward at the great pyramid.

I followed the direction of his outstretched arm. Once again joy surged through me.

Outlined in the sun atop the ancient stone were the small figures of two children hugging each other. Alone.

CHAPTER 26

We had promised to keep our distance from the slightest sign of danger. And this, I told myself, didn't seem to qualify as danger. Fred Jones was nowhere in sight.

Mike must have thought the same. Without saying a word, we both broke into a sprint. I reached the base of the pyramid a half step ahead of Mike.

What did the guidebooks say? Ninety-one steps to the temple that sat on top of the pyramids?

It seemed to take less than ten seconds. Yet as we scrambled upward, I puzzled.

How had Joel and Jessica made it to the top of the temple itself? The temple sat like a smaller box on a giant box, so that the pyramid was its base and provided a ten-foot-wide ledge all around. I remembered from a previous—and much more leisurely—climb that the temple rose at least another two stories from the top of the pyramid. Impossible that two small children should find a way to climb its sheer walls.

I found the answer to that impossibility at the end of our ninety-one steps. A ladder was on its side, lying against the wall of the temple.

Why had they climbed it? If they'd had this chance to escape Fred Jones, why had they chosen the pyramid instead of the hotel? Once there, why had they knocked the ladder over once at the top? In error, had their inexperienced minds told them it was a good way to keep Fred Jones from reaching them? Or had they accidentally knocked it over once on top?

I made the mistake of looking down, just as I had on the previous climb. I fought dizziness. Handling heights is not one of my strong points, and the steps stretched below me at a far steeper angle than any set of stairs.

Mike didn't notice my nervousness at our position.

"Quick," Mike said. He reached for the ladder and quickly leaned it against the wall. Its reach was just short of the edge of the temple roof. Mike began climbing and within seconds clambered onto the top of the temple.

I heard a cry of welcome from Joel. That was enough encouragement to get me over my jitters. I gritted my teeth and climbed. For a single heartbeat that felt like a year, the ladder tottered as I reached the final step at the top. Then it held, and I felt Mike's grip on my upper arm.

"I'm glad you decided to keep me company," he said softly. "It'll take both of us to get them down."

The softness of his tone told me that he had noticed my jitters. I was grateful he had not pointed it out and laughed at me.

I scanned the roof at our feet, careful not to look beyond its edges. Joel's teddy bear was at his feet. There was a small square bench of stone. Resting upon it was a statue of a parrot and several gold goblets. Beyond that, a bucket of something dark and a closed potato sack.

Despite our presence, Joel did not let go of Jessica. The poor guy was even more afraid of heights than I was. That realization should have told me something, but my own fear of heights pushed away a tiny voice in my head that was trying to make itself heard.

"How are we going to do it?" My voice quivered. I hadn't been able to avoid a quick glance away from Joel and Jessica. The jungle seemed terrifyingly too far below.

"No problem," Mike said with a confidence I hoped he felt.

He unbuckled his belt and pulled it loose.

"Do the same," he said.

I did.

"We'll loop the belts together, then beneath Joel's armpits. That way, one of us at the top can hold on while the other below guides his feet."

Jessica said something in quick Spanish.

"Sorry." I shook my head. "No comprendo."

She pointed at the edge of the jungle.

Then I understood. I understood what she had said. I understood why the ladder had been lying on its side against the wall of the temple. And I understood why Joel was up here despite his terror of heights.

They had been left here as prisoners.

How handy. The best guard of all was the two-story drop to the ledges below. With the ladder removed, Joel and Jessica would have no choice but to remain until their captor returned.

As he did now with two others.

For Jessica had pointed out three figures far below at the edge of the jungle, all running toward the pyramid.

I recognized one as Fred Jones. The others—two men who appeared to be Americans—I had never seen before.

"This isn't good," Mike said. "Stay low."

"No time to run," I agreed between tight lips. "They'll spot us in a second. We'll never get away before they reach the pyramid."

Stuck like legless bugs in a frying pan, I thought. The men halved their distance to the pyramid. *With the flame below the pan about to double the heat.*

Mike crawled to the edge of the temple, curled his hand over the edge, and made a slight movement. I could not contain my gasp of horror as I heard the results of that action. He had pushed the ladder away from the wall and let it fall onto the ledge below.

He answered my unspoken question. "Don't you think they'd be surprised to see the ladder in place when they get back? We can't escape here anyway. We can only hope they didn't hear the ladder fall. At least then we'll have the advantage of surprise when they get up here."

He caught the dismay on my face.

"Weapons?" Mike asked quickly. "Maybe the parrot statue."

His eyes flicked the area. "What about that sack?"

I stayed in a crouch as I moved. Partly not to be seen, but mainly because of my fear of falling off the roof. Then I nearly toppled over from surprise as I lifted the bag and met no resistance of weight.

It was as light as . . . feathers?

No time to mutter surprise. We heard low voices at the base of the great pyramid as the three men began to climb. I dropped the bag at my feet, and it landed with no sound.

An eternity later we heard a scrape near the edge of the roof.

Someone had just placed the ladder in position. We both fell flat on our stomachs. Joel and Jessica remained silent, staring first at us, then at the edge.

What had been done to them to terrify them into such total silence?

Slight thumps as one of the men moved upward.

What to do? I whispered the question to Mike.

"Push the ladder over and bean the others with the statue and loose rocks?" he asked.

I nodded.

Mike crawled halfway there. Then stopped and crawled back. When he looked at me, I caught a spasm of agony and sadness.

"I'm sorry," he whispered. "I couldn't do it. Not when I thought of what would happen to the guy. I'm really sorry."

I closed my eyes briefly and thought of what I'd so quickly agreed for Mike to do. To let him seriously hurt or maybe kill a man by cold-bloodedly pushing him off the side of this pyramid.

"My fault," I whispered back and wondered if my own regret showed on my face the same way his pain had.

The belts lay on the roof in front of our eyes. And a thought I didn't want to think rushed through my mind.

"Slight chance," I said with a muffled grunt. I reached for my belt. Then I scrabbled backward.

My stomach flipped at the news that was both good and bad.

At the top, unlike some of the stones partway up, the edges of the stone had worn so that there was a gap big enough to fit the belt buckle. But not enough so the buckle slipped through.

I glanced Mike's way. His widened eyes showed that he understood.

The thumps grew louder as the man neared the top.

I prayed the stone would hold the belt buckle in place, then prayed the leather of the belt would support my weight. I slid off the edge and held the end of the belt.

Everything held.

Because my eyes were closed, I felt—rather than saw—Mike beside me. Not a moment too soon. A snarl told me the man had arrived on the roof.

"Brats," rasped Fred Jones' voice. "It was much easier when I thought we could kill you up here."

My heart pounded so badly it seemed its movement inside my ribs would push me away from the wall. Directly below me was a ledge much too narrow for the distance I would fall before tumbling over beyond it down the steep sides of the pyramid like so many pounds of real-life rag doll.

Will the leather continue to hold? What if Jessica or Joel gives away our presence? Or if Jones happens to notice the shiny edges of our belt buckles? Or if one of his two companions happens to walk around the ledge and check our side of the temple walls?

All that fear kept the tiredness in my arms from reaching my brain. But only for the first minute.

The leather held. Jessica and Joel remained silent. Fred Jones didn't notice our belt buckles. And his two companions stayed on the side of the temple that held their ladder.

And now my arms threatened to betray me. *How much longer can I hold?* Each second became an hour.

A slight whimper from Joel.

"Shut up, kid. Lowering you on this rope's a lot better than what you were going to get."

Sudden anger drove away my fear and the numbing pain in my arms. Joel's only chance was me and Mike.

Finally I opened my eyes.

Mike's face was only inches away. By the glare of his eyes and the set of his jaw, I knew he, too, held the same anger.

"Ready for brat number two?" Jones called. "And keep a good grip on the girl down there. She nearly got away on me before."

Somewhere in the agony of waiting, he had lowered Jessica to the two men. Probably with the same rope he was now using on Joel.

Thinking of what might happen to Joel gave me the strength to hold on.

Another eternity of waiting. Then the sounds of Fred Jones climbing back down the ladder. Mike didn't hesitate. His face burning bright red with effort, he pulled himself up and flopped one hand over the edge to wedge his fingers into a crack on the roof between stones. That gave him enough grip to wiggle his way upward and back onto the roof.

I tried the same but couldn't find the strength.

"Do it, pal," he hissed. Mike grabbed both of my wrists from above.

It was painful, his pulling with me hanging downward. But it was a good pain, even if the skin on my inner arms peeled itself away as inch by inch I scraped my way upward.

Then I was there. With enough weight on top to wiggle forward.

I wanted to cry with relief.

But voices below froze me into swallowing any sobs.

"The teddy bear," another voice said. "Don't the sarge want to check the trace on its electronics?"

"Not much time," Jones said. "This place'll be crawling with tourists soon enough. We'll hide now and bail out tonight. If trouble hits us, these hostages will buy our getaway from whoever planted the bug."

"Sarge'll kill us if we don't bring it back."

The answering words crawled up my spine.

"Climb, then," Jones said. "Go back up, grab the stupid thing, and catch up to us."

That was it.

He climbed up.

And we had no place to hide.

We didn't even have the strength to scream for help.

Not that the energy would have done us much good when the face that appeared showed shock first, then recovered quickly enough to grimace with evil as its owner reached down for the gun that held us silent.

CHAPTER 27

We could only hope that Lisa and Ralphy might spot us from a distance as we were led away from the pyramid. Because there was no chance to resist. Not when Fred Jones had threatened to gladly shoot Joel if we slowed them in the slightest.

So we stayed ahead as they hurried all of us to the far edge of the jungle. They guided us to a path invisible from ten feet away. Only then did Fred Jones and his companions relax.

"Back to the work huts?" one asked Jones.

"Nope," Jones said. "Kay wanted a head start. He told us to meet him at the bat cave. Expect a long walk."

"And we do what the boss man says," the third man added.

Roderick Kay—boss man and sarge? Bat cave?

Something poked my kidney urgently. Not Jones' finger, but the barrel of his pistol. I stepped forward as directed by the gun, unhappily aware that the answers waited somewhere ahead in the jungle.

The bat cave was another cenote, smaller and shallower than the Sacred Well. One wall had collapsed into a pile of rubble. A path through that rubble showed many feet had walked to the bottom, where a stream trickled across an area of flat rock and disappeared into a giant hole in the opposite wall of the cenote.

An armed guard—American, with a flat black machine gun—acknowledged our arrival with a lazy wave.

"Move down," Jones said to me. "You've avoided anything cute so far. Now's a lousy time to try anything."

As if we could. We'd spent the last three hours walking and sweating and fighting jungle vines through a narrow path. My right foot now throbbed unbearably. I wanted to fall forward and plunge my head into the rusty-colored stream below.

What now? We were at least six miles from the hotel. Even given a month, there was no way an army of searching police could cover the area of a circle with a six-mile radius.

Roderick Kay was probably not in a good mood. He could not return to the hotel without being questioned, not with Fred Jones, his pilot, as the main suspect in a kidnapping that now included Mike and me. That meant whatever operation Kay was running was now probably over. Which did not seem to promise good things for us, his captives.

And even if we could escape, where would we go? I knew we'd never be able to find the route back. The compass in my back pocket seemed—as Lisa had always pointed out—useless. Knowing north wouldn't help in this jungle.

"Double-time," Jones snarled. For emphasis he pushed my back. Stumbling for balance on the steep downward path through the rubble effectively kept me from thoughts of future nastiness.

Roderick Kay stepped from the cave's shadows. He appeared completely different. No safari clothing. No bowed head for meekness. He wore camouflage pants, dark aviator sunglasses, an army cap. His shoulders were thrown straight back. He no longer seemed short. He projected power and anger with his rigid military posture.

"Jones, you'd be out of step in a one-man parade," he barked. "I told you to bring in two kids, not four."

"Sir, we were detected."

Kay looked Mike and me up and down. Nothing in his face betrayed his thoughts.

"These the ones who penetrated main base?"

"Yes, sir. And one other. The skinny one."

"Fool. If you'd only kept the door locked."

"I explained, sir," Jones whimpered. "I was only gone forty-five minutes. Their faces showed up on the security video, and I radioed ahead to you while they were walking back to the hotel."

Kay turned his dark glasses toward Jones. "Shut up. You were asleep in the hangar, afraid if you slept beside the jet I might catch you there. Repeating the excuse doesn't make it any better."

"Yes, sir." Jones saluted.

"You," Kay barked at the others. "Take these hostages inside."

They obeyed without speaking. We entered the coolness of the cave. Splattered in all directions were great piles of bat droppings.

A low hum reached us as we picked our way through. I understood after two more steps took us around a bend. Where the stream had worn the limestone through the centuries, the cave expanded to double in size, a large cavern that echoed the plinks of condensation water that fell from the roof.

The low hum was a gas-powered generator, one that provided electricity for the narrow string of bulbs that dimly lit one side of the cavern. I looked up first but could not even see if bats were roosting there in the darkness. I turned my attention ahead.

Military bunk beds lined the far wall, nearly a dozen sets. In front of those were rough wooden tables and rickety chairs. Plates and cutlery were set in perfect order on the tables, ready for a meal to arrive.

To the side of this living area were rows of long tables. It took me a moment in the dim light to recognize the objects on these tables; at first they appeared to be round-shouldered headless ghosts. But as my eyes adjusted, I saw instead they were birdcages—dozens upon dozens—shrouded with pale cloth.

Other nearby tables were surrounded by low stools. On these tables were some Mayan statuettes similar to the ones I remembered seeing near the private jet. Knives and other assorted unfamiliar tools rested alongside the statuettes.

A rattle of chain drew our attention. Mike and I stepped back, despite the guns pushing us forward. For it seemed as if zombies were rising toward us from the shadows!

"Jessica!" came the voice from one of the zombies. And my eyes quickly made another adjustment in this tricky light. The dark figures—shackled by chains—were a man and woman rushing to hold Jessica, who had broken away from us.

Spanish reached us, Spanish mixed with sobs of tears and happiness and sadness. The three of them formed a single figure.

And beyond that single figure were a dozen others, sitting motionless on a bench along the cavern wall. All with a length of chain shackled from ankle to ankle.

Jones and his two companions pushed us toward Jessica and her parents. They then pushed all of us toward the wall.

"Get comfortable," Jones said. "You'll be here awhile."

Joel kept a firm grip on my hand, and in a half-daze, we made our way to an open spot on the bench.

"Not so good, Señor Kidd, that you join us," the man beside me whispered. "These are desperate men with much to lose."

l turned my head upward to look at the face of the shackled Mexican who spoke English and somehow knew my name.

He nodded sadly as comprehension filled my face. "Yes," he said. "We, too, were taken as easily as a wolf takes a lamb."

It was the same federal officer who had questioned us the day before. His older partner sat beside him on the bench, staring at the ground.

CHAPTER 28

Mike was the one who finally broke the glum silence after Jones and his companions left us in the rear of the cave. He leaned across Joel and spoke to the officer beside me.

"A private jet at one place and now birdcages in a hidden cave," Mike said. "I don't get it."

The officer beside me—who had introduced himself as Carlos—lifted his head and slowly turned it sideways to gaze at Mike. His once proud mustache was now limp and greasy.

"Private jet?" he said in a voice filled with fatigue. "Inconceivable. In other words—"

"Please," Mike said. "I know what the word means. But why is it inconceivable?"

"Our authorities have searched this area again and again. Aside from the Chichén Itzá airport, there are no runways. Time and again we have made surprise inspections at that airport. No jet."

Mike started to explain, but curiosity made me interrupt.

"You were *looking* for a jet? That must mean . . ."

"It means long ago we suspected this area was a smuggling base," he said with the same tiredness. "We just couldn't pin who and how."

I thought of the artifacts and assorted tubes and birdcages that had lined the wall beside the jet and made the only guess I could. "Birds and statuettes?" I asked. "Why smuggle those?"

The older officer, Miguel, was now listening. "Big money,"

he answered. "Some of the parrots sleeping in those cages are worth ten grand."

"Ten thousand dollars?" I echoed.

"And our Mexican heritage—these statues, the ones that aren't fake—are worth hundreds of thousands to American collectors."

"Hold on," Mike protested. "Fake?"

"Some of the people on this bench are true craftsmen. They can carve an exact replica of the original, so true it would take a museum expert to tell the difference."

Then Miguel chuckled bitterly. "But these aren't smuggled to museums. The fakes go to private collectors instead, collectors scattered far enough apart and isolated from one another—not that they'd ever let it be publicly known they have these collections—so that they'll never know other collectors have identical fakes."

"So they are smuggling fakes out of the country because . . ."

"If it's smuggled, it seems more like an original," Miguel filled in for me. "It's a good scam. They make millions."

"But why not smuggle drugs?" I said. "Couldn't they make just as much that way?"

"Perhaps. But in drugs, there are wars for territory. Not with this. In drugs, a person might be executed if caught. Not with this. A slap on the wrist is all they would get."

"Except now we know about the kidnappings," Carlos said, "these Mayas who now live as slaves inside this cave. Some who are forced to make the carvings, and some who serve as hostages."

"Slaves!" Mike said. Joel, between us, listened intently and swung his short legs in the air below the bench. "These people have been trapped here?"

"The legend of Kukulcan, the feathered serpent," Carlos said. "Yesterday Roderick Kay stood in front of us here and bragged about everything."

Carlos explained it for us. The dig at the Sacred Well was just an excuse to be in the area. Roderick Kay had then begun to spread rumors about human slaves and the return of the legendary feathered Kukulcan, helped by occasional moonlight appearances of Fred Jones flitting through the jungle in a long, feather-covered cape.

These legends had been reinforced through the kidnapping of some of the local Mayan peasants, mainly those who refused to believe. The kidnappings had served several purposes. They had frightened the others into silence and belief. They had given Kay a workforce here in the cave. Once the legend had been whispered and rewhispered among the Mayas, it had encouraged others to begin delivering parrots, for Kukulcan it was said, wished the feathers and promised blessings or deliverance from Kukulcan in return.

The dig had served as the perfect area to receive the parrots from the Mayas, who knew the jungles well and could capture the birds from miles around.

Artifacts, too, were demanded by Kukulcan and were to be thrown into the Sacred Well. What the Mayas did not know was that, as head of the dig, it had been simple for Roderick Kay to stretch a wide net across the well, several feet below the water. Artifacts that had been kept hidden in the huts of Mayan families for untold generations were now gladly brought forth, and on moonlit nights they were sacrificed again to the Sacred Well, as it had been done by their ancestors centuries before.

These were later retrieved by Roderick Kay. Some—the ones of poorer quality—were used as proof that Señor Castillo's theory of artifacts buried near the well was correct. The other artifacts were replicated and smuggled into the United States.

"Yes," Carlos finished. "It was a perfect operation. All we had were suspicions."

He looked us up and down. "You see, our suspicions started when groups of Americans would disappear in this area. They'd arrive as tourists on a ten-day stay but would not leave the country for several months. Officials in immigration noticed a pattern.

"Always a group of six. Always a ten-day visit. When they looked closer, they discovered another pattern. All six had military backgrounds."

I looked at the far edges of the cavern. "Guards," I said. "Roderick Kay needed squads of men to guard his slaves."

Carlos nodded. "And to do the other things at night to keep the Mayas believing in Kukulcan."

Miguel continued. "Yes. But we had only suspicions. So we started monitoring the mail that left the dig."

Mike nodded satisfaction. "And you read the letter that included six tickets and expenses for a ten-day trip, the letter sent to Joel Kidd."

"The other Joel Kidd was expected by more than Señor Castillo," the mustached officer confirmed.

"Which explains," I said, "my brother, Joel, being stopped at customs. And also explains the conversation Mike and Ralphy and I overheard."

I told the officers about Roderick Kay's threat to Jones that others had better arrive immediately, the threat we had heard while hiding beside a garbage bin.

"Tell us more," Miguel said. "All of us have all day on the bench."

"I thought you said Kay made these people work," Mike said as he pointed at the tables that carried half-completed statuettes. "This coffee break'll end soon."

"No, my friend. I'm afraid not. You and the other little ones have wrecked the secrecy that was so vital to Roderick Kay. It would appear he is making plans to abandon this base."

"Great," I said. "So we've got to wait until he goes."

Miguel shook his head. "I'm afraid it will be much worse. Why leave any witnesses? So please, let us continue to talk; it will distract us from contemplating our fate."

CHAPTER 29

As we talked, Joel, restless without his teddy bear, swung his feet. My own, now shackled, still hurt, especially the top of my right foot. I reached down to massage it as Mike explained to the officers about our discovery of the jet.

They listened, asked for a complete description of the jet, and their faces finally showed animation.

"Long range, no doubt," Carlos said. "And Jones keeps the old red beater of a plane in sight to convince us nothing leaves the peninsula from here."

Miguel scratched his head thoughtfully. "Yet it must take great planning to choose the landing sites in the United States. There must be someone else to arrange that."

Before we could continue, a quick beat of heels against stone alerted us to a visitor. Roderick Kay—holding Joel's again-unstuffed teddy bear—marched straight to Mike and me.

"Answers," he said in a tight tone. "And now."

We nodded vigorously. It was easy to understand why this version of Roderick Kay scared Fred Jones so badly.

"An electronic homing device was planted in this teddy bear. Who put it there? Why?"

"I don't know," I said for Joel. I hoped my voice didn't sound as trembling as it felt.

"Look, brat. Jones was ready to tar and feather those kids and leave them hanging dead on the side of the pyramid." Kay paused and tapped his chin as he pretended to think. "No reason we can't do that to *four* of you tonight. That'll throw a real good scare into these Mayas."

I thought of the bucket of pitch and the lightness of the potato sack and understood. The sack held feathers. Jones had probably been on top of the pyramid, ready with Joel and Jessica as we first ran past it on the way to the Sacred Well. Until Jones had spotted the homing device inside the teddy bear. Joel's teddy bear had saved his life, but maybe only delayed the end so that it would occur in this cave.

"Speak," Kay ordered.

"We really don't know," Mike insisted.

Kay brought up his arm as if to strike us. Carlos said something in heated Spanish. Kay glared, spun on his heel, and left.

Carlos shrugged. "I merely asked him what he would gain to have all these adults beside me angry to the point of revolt should he strike someone so small. Would it be worth the trouble, I asked, even if he and the other Americans were armed."

Carlos smiled, happy at his small victory. "And I used Spanish so that all on the bench would hear and understand.

"I am intrigued," Carlos said now as his face became more serious. "We did not plant the bug. You certainly did not. Who?"

Miguel nodded. "And it is too bad that it was discovered. For it would have led that unknown person right to this cave. Our only chance for rescue."

I stopped massaging the top of my foot. Who had planted the bug? Maybe I knew. And maybe I knew when. And if I were right, I knew she was probably now on the way to this very cave.

I took a deep breath and told Carlos and Miguel my theory, a theory that filled all of us with hope as we waited.

That's why it broke our hearts to see—three hours later—the armed guards push Sofia ahead of them into the cavern.

CHAPTER 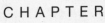 30

"We wondered when you would get here," I said glumly after the guards had shackled her among us and departed. "Only we hoped for rescue, not company."

Sofia raised her eyebrows. "You expected me?"

I pointed at my right shoe. "There's one disadvantage with planting a tiny homing device in someone's sneaker. Pain."

She raised her eyebrows higher. "Why you think a Maya with no education would do such a thing?"

Thing sounded like *theeng*. "Is that really your accent?" I asked.

She grinned. "Not at all. Tell me, how'd you guess?"

"Besides a sore foot? Roderick Kay told us about the homing device in Joel's teddy bear, and it struck me that whoever cared that much about our locations would probably plant more than one. Then my foot told me something I should have realized earlier. There was something wrong with my shoe, the same shoe that had given me no problems during all my walking in the first five days here. When I tried to figure out when it started to hurt, I remembered it was after we had had our talk. That made me wonder why you had been so careful to get me to follow Fred Jones. And I wondered why you had been so quick to disappear this morning when the rest of us went searching for Joel."

"Back to the hotel room to check my tracing monitors. Joel's had been destroyed. So I had to rely on yours. Getting a bug into his teddy bear was easy because it was in your hotel room. I was able to plant it before I met up with you and Jessica the other night. I was lucky that I could get your shoes that night in the hut."

I shrugged. "Not that it's done us any good now."

"More good than you realize," Sofia said, now in a faintly British accent. "And we have a little time. I'll explain."

She was Maya, of course, as she told us. But her parents were among the wealthy in the capital of Merida. She'd been sent to English boarding schools and educated in England with years of university. She was now a London professor of biology—concerned not with crimes like smuggling but with ecological movements. She had joined the International Council on Animal Preservation and discovered how the population of exotic parrots was being so badly depleted, almost in the backyard of her childhood. That led to a short-term agreement with the U.S. Fish and Wildlife Service, which badly wanted someone who could report from the Mexican interior without being noticed immediately as an outsider.

"And that's it," she finished brightly. "I was the perfect candidate. And I had no classes to teach in the summer. It didn't take long to hear those rumors about Kukulcan. So I got a job here as a waitress to find out more." She frowned. "When I heard about Jessica living in that hut with no parents, I adopted her as a niece, and it became even more important to me to find out what the truth was."

"But these electronic devices," Carlos protested. "You're a professor. Not an FBI agent."

Sofia laughed. "In London you can find dozens of shops that specialize in that sort of thing. Mostly electronic toys for adults who can afford it and like to think they need to be spies in business situations. For me, part of it was the game of now being a spy myself. So I wandered into a shop and they sold me lots of lovely things for me to use down here."

Her face darkened temporarily. "I didn't expect the kids to be endangered, though. If I hadn't planted that second bug . . ."

I wasn't sure if it would be a good time to remind her that she was now in as much trouble as we were.

"Why the kids?" Miguel asked. "Why not plant them on Fred Jones or Roderick Kay?"

"I did," she said, "or at least, I did *try*. But those guys are security freaks. The best I could do was plant some on their vehicles. But vehicles don't drive up to caves like this. And their old van just went back and forth to the airport."

"You tell her about the airport, Mike," I said. "I'm too depressed."

Mike explained briefly. Sofia then placed a hand on my arm.

"Cheer up," she said. "Everything has worked out fine so far. I needed you guys to be the unseen ones to lead me here. And—" she held out her hands with a broad grin—"I'm here."

"Great," I said without enthusiasm.

"Also, taking positions outside the cave are thirty policemen. All called in from Merida by your friend Ethel Bugsby."

I brightened. "You let them capture you as a diversion!"

"Exactly. And to be able to let you know exactly when the police will be storming the cave. Because in exactly—" she studied her watch—"fourteen minutes and thirty seconds, the fun begins."

Miguel shook his head and sighed. "You amateurs are very dangerous," he said slowly, then turned his eyes to stare directly into Sofia's. "You think you know it all. Our rescue is impossible. Roderick Kay is no fool. He lets all of his prisoners know one thing. He has two bundles of dynamite buried near the entrance, ready for the guards to set off should anyone try to escape. And when the dynamite explodes, boom, this whole cave collapses."

He consulted his own watch. "I think when your police make their move in thirteen minutes and fifty seconds, all of us will become very dead."

Thirteen minutes and fifty seconds translates to less than a thousand heartbeats, even if your heart is racing with fear like mine was.

A slight squeak reached us from high above in the darkness, so slight I could barely hear it above the pounding of my heart.

"A bat," Sofia whispered.

"This is no time to speak of bats," Carlos said quietly.

"What is different?" Sofia asked. "Of things of life and death? No, let us pretend the end will not arrive so soon."

"Bats?" I said, clutching at any subject except dynamite and the passing of seconds.

"Yes, it is a shame you haven't been at a place like this at dusk to see it," she said. "A cenote cave has hundreds of thousands of bats. When they fly out, it is a sight of magnificence that takes away your very breath."

I looked up again, although I'd probably already done so a dozen times and seen nothing.

"In these shadows," she smiled in response, "they will be invisible, wrapped in their wings of black leather. But at dusk, when they go to make their evening rounds, they fly out in columns. Dozens and dozens of columns. Thousands and thousands and unnumbered thousands of bats. So many, it would not have been worth Kay's while to keep them away. Instead, they share the cave."

As if hearing her, another bat squeaked.

She continued. "How do they fly with such precision, you might ask? Sound. They squeak in high pitches and wait for the sound to bounce off objects ahead of them. Much like radar."

I hardly heard her finish. My mind was on a single word. *Sound.*

Yes, I thought. *It might work. Sound!*

I grabbed Mike's knee.

"Hey," he said.

I ignored his indignation. "Tell me you have it with you. Your whistle."

"Yeah," he replied. "But it's a lousy time to call dogs or scare away snakes."

Then his eyes widened as he, too, understood.

We quickly explained to Sofia and Carlos. They grinned.

Sofia then turned to face everyone on the bench and spoke Spanish for several minutes. They stared back at her, stone-faced, and finally, as if on cue, all broke into broad grins.

"Two minutes remain," Sofia announced to us. "The police will rush the cave in two minutes, so I will begin in a minute and a half. This diversion *must* work. Be prepared to run then."

She focused on Mike and me. "You two, the ones without shackles, make sure the little ones do not become lost or confused."

She smiled calmly and accepted Mike's silent dog whistle. She studied her watch and waited for the seconds to pass. It seemed to take an hour until, without looking up from her watch, she began to blow.

There was, of course, no sound.

Yet seconds later, the first faint twitter reached us. Then another. And another. And bats began to fill the air.

They dropped like stones with wings. Black rain that blotted out the dim glow of the lights as they screamed and screeched and flew in circles of panic.

Within moments, it seemed as if we were in a howling, living blizzard. Bats collided with each other, then into us.

"Run!" Sofia shouted.

Joel gripped my hand as frantically and as tightly as I gripped his.

It was like wading into a dark snowstorm of blindness. Bats, barely larger than mice, bounced off our shoulders and lowered heads. I kept one arm in front of my face for protection and pulled Joel along with the other.

I didn't know I was yelling in rage and anger and in frustration at these thousands of creatures that flurried and swooped and screeched and howled in equal rage and anger and frustration.

It wasn't until daylight appeared in the background of the hundreds of hurtling black objects that I realized I was screaming. Or that we'd made it. Or that the dynamite hadn't exploded.

And it was a few days later that I found diamonds in the compass I'd been carrying the entire time.

CHAPTER 31

"And that's about the end of all that happened," I finished for Mad Eddie in Jamesville four days after stepping out of that cave into sunlight, and one hour after arriving back in town. "Mike's high-frequency dog whistle woke the bats and drove them crazy. Not only that, it messed up their radar systems. Sofia says it made it like a traffic jam for them, with all the cars going in all different directions at top speed. More than enough to distract the guards."

Mad Eddie didn't say much, just looked at me steadily from his wheelchair on the front porch of his house.

"When we made it out of the cave, all the police were waiting. The guards never had a chance. And nobody got hurt."

Still nothing from Mad Eddie.

"It was a happy ending," I said. "The Mayas returned to their families. And all of us are safe in Jamesville again."

Mad Eddie waited.

I was in no hurry, either. It was great to be home again. No sweltering heat. No jaguars or bats or snakes to worry about. Just a nice summer day with familiar bird sounds and the distant roar of a lawn mower. And me, calmly measuring each word as planned to deliver to the man in the wheelchair.

"You might have heard about the one problem, though," I went on. I wondered if he could detect any anger in my icy words. "Roderick Kay had long since escaped in his private jet. He'd told Fred Jones to wait at the cave, then never returned."

"How would I know?" he muttered. "You all just got back."

A cool breeze moved through the open front porch. It ruffled Mad Eddie's hair as it rested on his shoulders.

"Long-range fuel tanks," I said, as if I hadn't heard him. In my anger, I was relentless. "Fast-moving small jets like that can stay low and avoid any radar tracking systems. Roderick Kay could have landed just about anywhere in the United States."

I moved in front of Mad Eddie so he couldn't avoid my eyes.

"Where *did* he land?" I asked.

He stared at me without flinching. Stared longer and knew that I knew.

"Where did he land?" I repeated.

"That's my business," he said. "Don't stand there expecting me to start sniveling and crying and telling you I'm sorry."

He caught the shocked anger on my face.

"Stuff it," Mad Eddie said with a blaze of defiance. "I messed up. I'll take care of it my way. And don't bother threatening me with jail." He gestured at his wheelchair. "It can't be much worse than this."

"How dare you—" I stopped myself. Because I realized how I must have looked. Feet spread apart. Hands on my hips. The picture of self-righteous anger.

Suddenly I felt stupid and sad and silly and embarrassed all at once. Who was I to judge this guy? What did I know what it was like to live in a hated prison of a wheelchair after having the freedom to soar like a bird?

"I'm sorry," I said slowly. And I meant it. The speech I'd been practicing for the last couple of days would have been nothing more than a way of gloating over a troubled man and taking power from making him beg forgiveness. At that moment I could see myself in the glare of his eyes. I didn't like myself.

"I'm really sorry." Did he understand the apology was more to me? "Here's your compass," I then said as I pulled it from my pocket. "I kept it for Joel most of the trip."

His eyes widened completely, and he made a strangling sound in the back of his throat. I tightened my lips in sympathy at what I knew he suddenly knew. "May I sit down?" I asked.

"Yeah. Go ahead." Defiance was gone. Replaced by tiredness.

"They never got the note," he said as I took the weight off my feet. It was a statement, not a question.

"No."

"Nor the diamonds." Mad Eddie's voice drifted toward my back as, from his top step, I leaned over my knees and stared ahead at the tree in his front yard.

"Nor the diamonds." The faraway lawn mower suddenly shut down and magnified the silence between us. I thought of how I'd dropped the compass after our trip and then heard the rattle of something loose inside as I picked it up.

"You guys could have been killed," Mad Eddie said. "Joel too."

"Something like that," I said. Why did I feel so sad at the pain in his voice? Minutes ago I had wanted to strangle him.

"I hadn't planned it that way."

Now I really wanted to cry. He wasn't blaming me for keeping the compass. He was accepting the blame himself.

"How did you know?" he said heavily.

"Jones told us a lot after. Plus little things," I said. "Head lice. Getting caught in boxer shorts. Stuff like that."

Not even my attempt at humor cheered him.

"I don't get you," he said. "Head lice?"

"I woke up real groggy my first morning there," I said quickly. "So groggy that I didn't realize I hadn't dressed before answering the door. So groggy that anybody could have searched my room and not woken me up. Turns out Kay had slipped drugs into our food the night before, making us groggy so he could search our rooms. But it was dark and he mixed our stuff up."

I rubbed my head, remembering the lice. "Jones has a bad temper. When he searched our room, he ripped the teddy bear apart. Kay told him to fix it so no one would know they'd been in our rooms. Jones went to a maintenance room and sewed it, and no one noticed because the customs people had taken it apart already. Except when Jones stuffed it, he threw in some dirty scrap rags, and the lice hatched a few days later."

I put my hands in my lap again. "Jones never told us what he was looking for. When I found the diamonds, I understood. If he couldn't have them, he didn't want anyone else to have them."

I slid sideways so that I could still sit and lean against the porch railing but at least look back at Mad Eddie. His face was no longer tight with anger.

"Why was it, I had to ask myself, that Kay and Jones thought we had something they wanted. Why, unless we really *were* the Joel Kidd and party they expected. Just not *what* they expected."

Mad Eddie nodded.

"And who, I asked myself a little later, did we know that they might know? It was an obvious guess then. Former military people. A pilot. So are you. And there was one strange remark you made before we left. You asked if I'd ever flown anything other than a commercial jet. You told me it would be a thrill to be in a smaller plane. And it was. But how could you have known we would be in a smaller plane unless you knew Fred Jones would be our pilot?"

Mad Eddie nodded again, then told me what I had only been able to guess at. "I owed Roderick Kay. The guy saved my life once in the Gulf War. So when he asked me to be a stateside go-between for a smuggling operation, I said yes. It wasn't drugs, I told myself, plus I owed the guy. I'd set up the drop points by telephone; Jones would fly in, fly out. I'd also handle the money end. Collect money here and put it into a Swiss bank account, or sometimes find a way to smuggle them cash or diamonds if they wanted it delivered back to Mexico."

It was my turn to nod.

"Señor Castillo never existed," Mad Eddie said. "Some guy in military computers in Washington owed Kay favors. So the guy built a complete and fictitious background for a brilliant war vet and university grad turned archaeologist named Eduardo Castillo. When Mexican officials sent for confirmation before allowing the dig and giving grant money, everything seemed legit. Kay posed as second-in-command, and tried to appear afraid of everybody, especially Señor Castillo. He often told me by phone it was the perfect base."

I started to laugh. It caught and I couldn't stop. When I finally did stop, Mad Eddie was glaring with suspicion, as if he feared I was mocking him. "It's nothing," I said. "It's just that it probably was the perfect base. Until Joel showed up."

Mad Eddie smiled. "Joel. I like that kid. One day Kay insisted I get yet another crew together. About that time I was getting tired of all of this, arranging drop-off points and buyers and squads to go in every couple of months. Plus I'd heard rumors about the direction of the operation, and I didn't like it. I figured to kill two birds with one stone. Send the diamonds in the compass, along with a retirement note—and play a joke on them while giving your brother a great summer vacation. I mean, I knew even Roderick Kay wouldn't hurt innocent kids."

I took a deep breath. "You're probably right. Except he never got the note. Nor the diamonds. I had the compass all along. And the night they searched my hotel room was the night I had accidentally dropped it behind my dresser."

"You'll agree," Mad Eddie said, "that I didn't really mean for you guys to be in danger. If they'd found the compass..."

"... we would have been fine," I said.

But none of the rest would have happened. And the Mayas would still be trapped in that cave.

Mad Eddie wheeled forward. "I'm not good at asking for things," he said. "But it's important to me that you understand I didn't mean to risk any of you. Especially Joel."

I closed my eyes and spoke aloud what I'd memorized of the note after unscrewing the base of the compass. *"Rod. Here's the diamonds. You'll find extra from my own proceeds to cover the cost of these kids showing up. Hope you understand the unwritten message, too. I want out and I won't arrange any more squads for you."*

"You do understand?"

I said I did. But what to do about Roderick Kay? And the diamonds, which were, after all, blood money from the proceeds of a smuggling operation that used false beliefs to terrorize people.

I didn't want to look like I was judging Mad Eddie or blackmailing him into making things right. I shouldn't have worried.

Mad Eddie took care of half of it right away. "The diamonds you found," he said, "can you send them along to that ecology organization? This Sofia should know how to see that the money goes a long way."

"Sure," I said.

"Watch the newspapers for the rest," he said.

And that was it.

Two weeks later, as I helped push Mad Eddie to Leighton Hill for another kite-flying hour with Joel, he handed me a clipping from a Washington newspaper, which described the capture of an internationally wanted smuggler who had been located thanks to an anonymous tip.

He said little else to me, ever. Just the four usual sentences.

"Leighton Hill, kid," he'd say as Joel and I showed up. Then on top of Leighton Hill he'd say, "Far 'nuff, grunt. Leave me with sport here." And after a few seconds, "Come back in an hour."

Except now, long after that day, I was able to imagine that I'd seen a smile somewhere in that deep beard.

Because of that, I wish this story about kites, Sunday School cards, a spooky ten days in Mexico, and instinct would have ended there.

Instead, it ended in September.

Epilogue

Where the instinct comes in makes me believe what Dad told me about it. Of course, when he told me, it was at a time when all of us were ready to believe that explanation.

You see, the last time that Mad Eddie went flying with Joel and his teddy bear, he finally spoke more than four sentences to me.

The wind was blowing nicely, and Eddie's voice seemed a little softer. "Take the kid back with you," he said quietly. "He's already agreed to let the teddy bear stay with me."

That was something. It usually takes skilled deception to pry Joel from the teddy bear. Especially after all it survived in Mexico.

"And take your time coming back," Mad Eddie said.

As I was turning and Mad Eddie was lifting the kite from his lap, I glimpsed both of Joel's Sunday School cards, the ones from the first time they flew a kite together.

Each card is now high in my closet where I'm sure they'll never get lost. They were the kind with verses printed on and a drawing for the kids to color. One had Joel's scrawl all over it. "Jesus loves you, Mr. Eddie," it said in orange crayon. The other card had a drawing of someone flying a kite—colored in yellow and purple and green, and Joel hadn't stayed inside the lines anywhere—with the verse below it from 2 Corinthians that read, "Now the Lord is the Spirit, and where the Spirit of the Lord is, there is freedom."

How did Joel know to give him those cards, ones that would mean the most to Mad Eddie? And how did Joel know it would be the last time Mad Eddie would ever take him kite flying?

That's the part about instinct I can't answer. You see, when we walked back up the hill, Joel wasn't surprised to see Mad Eddie slumped over in the wheelchair, with the kite string tied to one wheel and his teddy bear on the ground where it had fallen. Joel didn't panic or become alarmed when I ran as hard as I could to find a doctor. He just waited beside the wheelchair and smiled at the doctor when he arrived at the top of the hill.

And how did Mad Eddie know which Sunday afternoon would be the day he could really fly and leave his wheelchair behind, along with the Bible they found in his jacket?

I can't answer that, either.

All I know is how Dad explained instinct to me the following Wednesday afternoon when we attended Mad Eddie's funeral.

"Instinct?" he whispered as Mom placed flowers in front of the fresh grave. "It's God's way of protecting His creatures."

The breeze around us quickened. It wasn't hard to guess what Joel was thinking as he watched the wind pluck petals loose and carry them high and soaring with freedom into the blue above us.